"Hear you call yourself a shootist, old man," sneered Blackstone, the Peacemaker with its polished barrel and engraved chamber casual in his gloved right hand. Gloves! So many of the kids thought it was smart to wear gloves like the flashy gunmen in the penny magazines they read.

"Go away, boy. Now and for good."

"You threatenin' me, old-timer?"

"No."

"Then . . .?"

"A promise, boy. Not a threat. A promise."

There'd been plenty of times when Jed Herne had been feeling more benevolent, and he'd let kids like Seamus Blackstone walk away alive. But he wasn't in the mood for charity right then . . .

Also by John J. McLaglen

and published by Corgi Books

Herne the Hunter 19: Bloodline

John J. McLaglen

CORGI BOOKS
A DIVISION OF TRANSWORLD PUBLISHERS LTD

HERNE THE HUNTER 19: BLOODLINE

A CORGI BOOK 0 552 11990 3

First publication in Great Britain

PRINTING HISTORY
Corgi edition published 1982

This book is set in 10/11 pt Paladium

Corgi Books are published by
Transworld Publishers Ltd.,
Century House, 61–63 Uxbridge Road,
Ealing, London, W5 5SA

Made and printed in Great Britain by
Hunt Barnard Printing Ltd., Aylesbury, Bucks.

This is for Clare, who makes beautiful things in glass and who vanished for entirely too long. I hope she doesn't disappear again. With love and all good things for the future.

"More often than not the old are uncontrollable. It is their tempers that make them so difficult to deal with."
Euripedes

1

Jed Herne couldn't remember being in so much damned pain.

In his forty-three years of living there was hardly a part of his body that had escaped injury. He'd been stabbed with knives and war-lances. Shot at and occasionally hit with guns of every calibre known to man. Punched and kicked by a variety of people, running from a twelve-year-old whore in Juarez one rainy Easter-time to a ninety-three-year-old Episcopalian bishop in Seattle. Admittedly the bishop had been defrocked for more than thirty-five years at the time of the incident.

Jed had come close to being burned alive and frozen and drowned. Once all on the same day.

It had been up in Montana. Eight or nine years back. A bitter January day with the cold so intense that a man's spittle sang in the air, ice before it hit the snow. Jed had been holed up in a small cabin used by line-riders, waiting out a blizzard. There'd been trouble in the nearby town of Wolf's Jaw, with a man shot in the shoulder and another clubbed unconscious. The fight hadn't been any of Herne's choosing, but the name of Herne the Hunter had travelled wide and the local good old boys had taken it into their heads to try and teach the stranger a lesson.

They weren't fast enough.

Not by a country mile.

Jed had been feeling generous and didn't kill any of them. But afterwards he'd regretted it. If you have a man down, then keep them down. Was it Josiah Hedges

9

who'd said that?

It didn't much matter.

What mattered was that they'd come out after him. Their pride so badly hurt that they'd braved the cold and the snow to ride out to the cabin. Opening fire with a fusillade of bullets that tore strips off the logs and shattered the window that looked out across the open ground.

There was a second window round back, opening out on the banks of the frozen river. There'd been a thaw a few days previously and the ice was opaque, pale blue, barely thick enough to carry a starving dog. The locals knew that whatever else happened Herne surely wasn't going to leave that way.

He held them off until dusk came creeping in across the frozen land, bringing with it a shimmering mist that made it hard for them to make out what was happening. Two of them tried to rush the front door under cover of that ghostly fog, but Herne could see out a whole lot better than they could see in and both of them died within seconds of each other. One with a fifty calibre ball through the brain and the other with a thirty-six through the throat, sending him kicking in the trampled snow that quickly turned scarlet.

While the rest of them waited in an angry silence, Jed made his move. Creeping away from the front of the cabin, towards the rear window.

But they still nearly caught him.

One of them took a chance and dashed in low, stumbling and nearly dropping the can of lamp-oil that he gripped in his gloved right hand. Lying panting beneath one of the windows, his breath pluming around his face. Splashing the oil over the logs, then rolling away and flicking a lighted match.

There was a dull whooshing sound that carried to Herne's ears and he returned to the front to see a wall of fire shooting up, blinding the window. Two of the other local men saw their chance and ran in with more of the pungent liquid, throwing it over the door, up high on the sod roof.

The flames licked eagerly at the new supply of oil and Herne could see nothing but bright fire. Breathe choking smoke that billowed in through the broken glass and around the ill-fitting door. Within five or ten minutes the whole place would be ablaze, the door gone, the roof catching. He already knew that there were around eight or nine guns still alive out in the cold snow.

'You got no chance and a slim chance, then you take the slim one.' That had been one of his old friend's sayings. Whitey Coburn, the tall, skinny albino who'd shared so many of the best and worst times with Jedediah.*

'Come out you bastard so we can hang you!'

'Cut his son-of-a-bitchin' cock off!' came another voice.

Bullets hissed through the flames, shattering a small mirror on the far wall of the cabin. It was beginning to get warm. Herne crawled back away from the front of the little building, keeping low. Cautiously lifting his head and peering through the broken window that overlooked the frozen stream.

'Slim,' he said quietly to himself.

There was so much smoke around that he knew the hunters outside couldn't possibly see him. He eased the latch on the window and opened it. Standing and holstering his pistol. Checking the retaining thong was over the top of the spurred hammer to keep it in place.

He remembered how he'd taken the heavy Sharps rifle and hurled it across the ice, as far as he could. Seeing it land half in and half out of the river, on its further bank.

No point in waiting. Already fire was snaking across the dry boards of the floor, lapping at the heels of his boots.

*For many of these good and bad times see the earlier adventures of Herne the Hunter, published by Transworld and listed at the beginning of this volume.

Minutes had become seconds.

Herne climbed on the dusty sill and dived clumsily out in a half crouch. Hoping that the ice might bear his weight if he rolled as he hit it.

It didn't.

There was a moment of resistance that jarred his shoulder and then a whispering crackle. Then the ice opened around him and he slid beneath the water as easily as a seal escaping from a polar bear.

The melt-water was going to be cold; he'd known that. But not such a biting, savage cold that it took every vestige of breath from his body and he gulped in a great mouthful of the surging stream. It was running fast – one of the reasons that the ice wasn't thicker, and he felt himself bowled along, tumbling against sharp boulders on the bed of the stream.

If he didn't get air fast then it was going to be over. He pushed upwards, lungs tight with pain. Feeling the ice with outstretched fingers that were already becoming numb.

He had edged himself sideways, towards the further bank, trying to reach up and break his way clear through the shuttering ice. But the current still moved him and he wasn't able to bring any pressure to bear. Twice he tried to punch through the dark barrier and twice his fist slid away. Though the ice wasn't strong enough to bear the weight of a man, it was too strong for Herne to batter his way through.

In a quieter part of the water he brought his face up close to the ice, chest straining with the effort not to open his mouth and inhale more water. But the pain was swelling and he knew that he was as close to death as he would ever be; ever could be.

'Air,' he panted, suddenly finding that there was a slim gap between the water and the bottom of the ice. Barely an inch and a half, it was enough for him to lift his head and draw in a partial breath, easing the pressure on his lungs.

But it would only be a temporary respite. The water was so cold that already his limbs were weakening. He had to break through. Had to.

There was only one hope, though the odds were against it. He reached down, still trying to kick his legs and keep himself afloat, face grazing the rough ice. Tugging off the leather thong and drawing the Colt Navy. His fingers were now frozen and he couldn't properly feel the familiar shape of the polished butt. But it was there, gripped tight.

If he dropped it , . .

His mind was going, sliding into blackness. There was a pushing behind the eyes and his stomach was tight with tension. Had he thumbed back the hammer? He couldn't tell. Couldn't feel the hammer.

The trigger.

Squeezed it.

Nothing. No noise. No concussion.

Nothing.

He'd sealed off the charges with grease, like he always did. And each ball fitted so tight that a tiny crescent sliver of lead was always peeled off as he rammed it home. The caps were tight-fitted.

The hammer . . . trigger . . . again.

His ears hurt at the shock of the explosion, only inches away from his face. Fighting to stay in the same position he pulled the trigger again, pressing the muzzle against the underside of the dark, slick ice.

A second time the gun misfired.

And a third.

That was about it. With a last, despairing effort Herne punched up with the pistol, hitting the ice. Feeling it give, weakened by the single bullet. He lashed out once more and his head was in the fresh night air.

Clawing out, hanging on the edge of the frozen river with his arms, drawing in great gulps of oxygen.

Herne had drifted around fifty yards downstream, and he could see the cabin, still blazing brightly, the roof well

13

alight. A couple of shadows moved dimly around it and he ducked below the water. Taking a deep breath and then powering himself up and to the side, feeling the ice creak as he stretched across it.

A few moments later he'd been safe.

He'd crawled back upstream in the cover of the brush, retrieving the Sharps. Shivering with the cold, knowing that death could still take him.

Ironically it had been the same fire that his would-be killers had set that saved him. Thinking that he must be dead they'd ridden triumphantly away, leaving the flames still high and red.

Hot enough for Herne to dry himself out and get good and warm for the long walk back into town. Where he'd stolen a horse and killed two of the men who'd hunted him.

But that had been times past, hardly worth the forgetting.

The new pain was something else. It had been settled in his jaw for weeks now.*

There'd been a travelling quack with a medicine show a few days back who'd offered to draw it for him. But the man had been so far gone in liquor that he'd looked at Herne through glazed eyes and asked him whether it was him or his twin brother who wanted the offending molar pulling.

By now Jed had decided that the bad tooth was maybe one of the big wisdom teeth at the back, top, right. His face was slightly swollen and he found that he could no longer chew jerky on that side of his face. If he could have reached it he'd have pulled it himself, but each time he tried his fingers slipped off the smooth tooth and it just hurt more.

Maybe there'd be someone to pull the tooth for him in the next township along the line. It was around a half mile to Stow Wells. A small community on the banks of

*See *Dying Ways*, the previous adventure in the best-selling series.

the San Simeon Creek, an off-shoot of the bigger Gila River. In the centre of the Arizona Territory. From what Herne recalled of Stow Wells it had been a pretty community, well-irrigated and green among the rolling orange wilderness all around it.

The summer sun floated serene and untroubled almost immediately overhead, sending most living things scuttling for the portions of shade beneath rocks. Herne reined in the big stallion and reached for the canteen. Tugging the cork out between finger and thumb and taking a single swig of the warm, brackish water, rolling it around his mouth and spitting it out where it vanished in the red dust. Drawing in one more mouthful and swallowing it, then replacing the cork and hanging the canteen back on the side of the saddle. Heeling the horse slowly onwards again.

He came over a low ridge and saw the settlement laid out beneath him, neat and pretty. The row of houses and stores in the main street as he remembered it. But there was a new farm out yonder. A mile or so to the north of Stow Wells, on a clearly-marked side-trail. But it wasn't a farm. There was little sign of stock. No more than a dozen head of cattle. Three or four horses. Just a patchwork of trim paths that wound among some green lawns, with a large, rectangular white building, single-storied, at its centre.

It looked more like a private house on a grand scale. Jed shaded his eyes with the flat of his hand, peering out and down, making out a few figures moving slowly around the grounds. But not able to see who they were or what they were doing.

'Guess I'll have to wait to find out,' he said to himself.

A couple of hundreds yards further on and Herne was riding slowly along the flat part of the trail, the houses of Stow Wells shimmering through the heat-haze. To one side of the rutted roadway he saw three figures. Hunched and bent, each one dressed in dark blue pants and a

15

cream shirt with loose sleeves. As he closed on them the shootist saw that they were all old men. Faces turning blankly towards the sound of his horse's hooves.

'Howdy,' said Jed, tipping his hat.

'Fuck you, stranger,' replied the nearest, drawing a battered Walker Colt from the back of his pants and cocking it. Aiming at Herne.

2

Herne's first reaction was to slide down from the saddle, drawing his own Peacemaker and putting a forty-five ball between the murderous old man's eyes. That would have been safest and easiest and Jed usually tried to follow those twin paths.

But he noticed that the barrel of the rusty pistol was shaking like a willow in a cyclone. And the other two old-timers were nudging each other and grinning.

Slowly a narrow, cold smile eased its way onto Herne's lips and he sat back calmly, rubbing his fingers inside his kerchief. Fixing his deep-set eyes on the face of the man with the gun.

'You put that handgun away, now.'

'What's that, stranger?'

'Yeah. Got to speak up, son. Ben here ain't so good at hearin' as he was.'

'That's a damned fact, Mister,' added the third.

'I said to put the gun up,' said Herne, raising his voice a little. Eyes never leaving the face of the first of the ancient trio.

'Why don't you make me, cowboy?' was the cackling reply. Delivered to the accompaniment of a thread of dark brown spittle that inched from the corner of the slack lips.

'I'm takin' it slow, old-timer. Fact is that I'm minded . . . truly minded to get down and take that heap of shit you're holdin' and ram it clean up your ass.'

There was a chilling intensity to the words that penetrated to all three of the old men and they stood, shocked into silence. Watching the stranger, realising that they'd surely picked on a loser for their joshing.

'We didn't mean nothin, Mister,' mumbled the one called Ben, holstering the pistol.

'Cemeteries full of mindless bastards that didn't mean nothing,' said Herne.

'His pistol ain't even loaded, stranger,' said the second of the old-timers, reaching down nervously and scratching at his stomach. His voice was shaking with shock.

'I don't give a sweet damn 'bout that,' replied Jed. 'Times past I'd have killed him just for lookin' like he was goin' to draw on me. He's lucky.'

'Hang on there a moment. Guess we owe you a sorry, Mister. . . . What's your name?'

'Herne. Jedediah Herne.'

The name got a reaction. He was used to that. But it wasn't the reaction that he expected. There was something else there. Not shock or fear. More an oddly coy interest.

'Herne the Hunter?'

Overlapped with: 'Jedediah Travis Herne?'

'That's what they call me.'

'Top shootist?'

Herne nodded. 'What's it to you?'

They all shook their heads like a row of toy owls, nudging each other as though they shared some private joke. 'Nothin', Mister Herne. Nothin' in this wide, wide world. Nothin'.'

'Wait until Al hears 'bout . . .' began one of them, only to be shushed into silence by the other two.

'Al. Who's Al?' asked the shootist.

'Al? He ain't nobody. Just one of us from the Home.'

'Home?'

'Sure. The Colonel Roderick Abernathy Home for Distressed Gentlemen,' replied Ben. 'Kind of a decent place.'

'The big white house to the north of town?'

18

'That's it. Colonel Abernathy's widow, Miss Lily, built it like he wanted from his money.'

'How many of you there?'

'That's hard to say. Lot of comin' and goin', if'n you take my meaning, Mister Herne.'

'Can't say I do.'

'Some arrives. Sent by other charities. But every now and again one of us gets us transmitted to the realms eternal.'

'Oh. You mean there's deaths.'

Ben shook his head so hard that Herne feared for his health. 'Not a word Miss Lily likes to hear. Makes it sound too overmuch like losin'.'

'Losing?'

'Al says that even losers get to be lucky some of the time,' said the second of the old men, nodding as if he'd just delivered himself of one of the great truths of infinity.

'Al sounds like some kind of a prophet,' grinned Herne, relaxing. Even forgetting the pain in his jaw for a few moments.

'Al's a real dumb asshole,' snapped the third of the oldsters.

'Hey, now . . . That ain't rightly fair, Paddy, and you know it,' retorted Ben.

'No it ain't. Half the time he doesn't even know who he is. Forgets to go to the necessary and messes his breeches. And those lyin' stories he makes about . . .'

'Hush up!' shouted Ben. 'Or I'll draw this here pistol and blow your brains out your neck.'

'Ben's right, Paddy,' calmed the third man, whose name Jed hadn't heard. 'Al's had him some bad times. We know that. And Mister Herne here won't want to hear about Al's little tales. He just up and makes them to keep himself contented, Mister.'

The shootist waved a hand. 'I understand. Don't worry none. Hey, this sure seems a nice place.'

'It is. Sure is. Been some trouble with Indians, though.'

'Chiricahua?'

Ben nodded. 'Bastards. I'd shoot every last mother-fuckin' son down and leave 'em rot.'

Herne sniffed. The pain was back. 'Anyone in town pull teeth? A doctor?'

Paddy looked at the other two. 'No. Guess not. Had a doctor at the Home. Good man. Doc Howell. Hear he took the last train for the coast. Now there's nobody. Matron says there'll be someone along next month.'

'Maybe,' interrupted Ben.

'Yeah. Maybe. But Matron isn't given to tellin' anythin' but the truth.'

'So who'd . . .?'

'Pull a tooth? We go to the smith. Big Jim Bisset. Does 'em sweet and easy and you get a slug of liquor on the house.'

'Charges two bits for a straight tooth. Dollar if'n he has to dig it out.'

'Sounds like my man. I thank you, gentlemen,' said Herne, doffing his hat.

'Good day to you, Mister Herne.'

'Yeah, good day.'

'You take care how you go, now. Watch out for some of them young whippersnappers that hang around the "Inside Straight" saloon,' warned Ben. 'Uppity kids filled with gall and no backbone.'

Paddy nodded his agreement. 'Seamus Blackstone's the worst. Red-haired boy. Watch for him. Figures all strangers are fair game for some sportin'.'

'Appreciate the warning.'

He heeled his horse on again, leaving the three old men behind. Pausing as he entered Stow Wells and looking back, seeing that the elderly trio was still where it had been. All three faces still turned to watch him go.

Herne cantered along the main street of the small settlement – the only street – past a half-built church. It was odd how many settlements in the South-west had

20

begun building the house of God in their midst and never somehow gotten around to completing it.

Drapes twitched at windows and he saw shadowed faces behind shimmering glass. It was the usual reception to anyone new in a far-away place and it didn't bother him. It would have bothered him more if folks hadn't taken any notice at all of him.

He passed the Sheriff's office, ignoring the lean man who was stretched back in a battered hickory rocking-chair, whittling on a piece of wood. The Arizona sun flickered off the silver star that was pinned to the man's vest. Herne was conscious of the attention he was receiving and it was no surprise when he glanced behind him and saw the chair was rocking gently on its own. And the door to the lawman's office stood open. The Sheriff would be inside, flicking through the latest pile of 'Wanted' flyers to see if there was anyone fitting the description of the shootist.

'Tall, broad in the shoulder. Aged around forty. Average weight. Hair long and greying at the temple. Dresses in ordinary clothes. No distinctive facial scars. Carries Colt Peacemaker and Sharps fifty calibre long gun.'

But there wouldn't be any flyers out. Herne knew this. Sure there'd been times gone when he'd crossed that thin, invisible line that set the orderly apart from the lawless. But right now he wasn't wanted in any state.

The smithy was just ahead of him, right next to the livery stables. Even in the burning heat of the day Herne could make out the glowing fire near the door, and the enormous figure of what he guessed must be Big Jim Bisset, arms folded, looking out into the street. The gnawing agony of the bad tooth seemed to suddenly ease away to nothing now he had reached the moment of having it actually drawn. But he was still going to go through with it.

When he caught the sound of horses behind him. And a rig, moving fast.

Someone yelling.

A scream.

Pounding hooves on the trail. And more shouting. The words inaudible.

The blacksmith came out into the light, blinking and shading his eyes with his sinewy, spark-scorched fingers. Herne swung in the saddle and looked back along the street.

Doors were opening, people stepping out on the high boardwalk, all eyes turned to look to the west. Wrapped in a soaring veil of reddish dust Herne could make out the lines of a Concord coach, rattling and pitching as the team of four horses pulled it at a frantic gallop.

And there was nobody up on the box.

The lean man that Herne had taken to be the law around Stow Wells ran out into the street, waving his hat and yelling to try and check the stampeding team. But they were on their way through, spooked beyond the furthest edge of panic, and it was going to take a lot to stop them. They slowed a mite and swerved around the Sheriff, but their progress was hardly impeded at all.

'Halt them! For Christ's sake hold them!!' came the yell and Herne saw the blacksmith take a few steps forward, then think better of it and stay where he was. Four galloping horses and a runaway stagecoach weren't going to be halted by one man with his bare hands.

Jed patted the neck of his own horse, gentling it and keeping it quiet among the building chaos. He reached down and thumbed the leather thong off the hammer of the pistol, so that it was free to draw.

'Stop them, Mister!' shouted the lawman, standing helplessly in the street as the team charged by him.

'Sure,' said Herne.

The single action pistol slid easily into Jed's hand, feeling just like an extension of his right arm. It was totally automatic to cock the gun with his thumb, index finger moving to the narrow trigger.

The first bullet hit the offside leader through the chest,

22

followed a fraction of frozen time later by a similar shot through the throat of the nearside animal. Herne could easily have shot the galloping horses through the head and brought them down instantly, but that would have produced a bloody shambles of an accident that would have turned the Concord and wrecked it. Killing anyone there might be left alive inside.

By shooting them in the body he'd slowed them immediately and brought them to a canter. Two more bullets and the coach was creaking to a halt. The two wounded animals were both crying out in shock and pain, whinnying high and clear through the bright sunlight.

A hundred paces down the trail, at the further edge of Stow Wells, and they had both stopped. One sinking to its knees with vivid blood pattering softly in the dust from neck and chest. The other still standing patiently in the traces, eyes rolling, sweat lathering its flanks and mingling pink with the dashed blood from its lungs.

Behind him Herne could hear cries and shouting, some sounding angry. Mostly upset and frightened. The lawman was running towards the stranded stage, pistol out in his hand.

'Mite late for the gun, Sheriff!' called the shootist, digging his short spurs into the stallion, walking it towards the coach.

It seemed as though most of the rest of Stow Wells was out in the street.

Jed swung himself down from the saddle, letting the reins dangle. Standing a moment and looking up at the dusty Concord. Noting the smears of fresh blood on the edge of the driver's seat. A scattergun still bucketed on the far side. A palm-print dabbed crimson on the near door. Several bullet-holes dotted the rear and the heavy oilcloth flap that was normally tied down over passengers' luggage had been slashed to ribbons.

The calling had died away behind Herne and all he could hear was the crunching of feet and the faint sound of a light wind rattling a loose shingle on the nearest frame house.

'Anyone livin', Mister?' called the Sheriff.

Herne stepped in closer and reached for the handle of the coach, feeling it sticky to the touch. Turning it and pulling the door open.

There was nobody living.

All he saw was a scalped and eyeless head, rolling gently on the floor of the stage.

No body.

Just the head.

3

'Course it was damned Indians!'

'I'm just sayin', Sheriff, that it could be renegades or a bunch of breeds. Even a gang of Mex bandits from south 'cross the River.'

The law in Stow Wells, Arizona Territory, was a young-looking forty-year-old; Sheriff Clifford V. Williamson. Son of a local rancher, he'd been the law for close on twenty years. The settlement was generally quiet and the slaughter of the coach's passengers, driver and shotgun had left him shocked and angry.

'Indians,' repeated Williamson, stubbornly. 'Scalpin' and butcherin' like that. Chiricahua. Under Mendez. Small sub-tribe.'

'Not normally the Apache way . . . taking a stage like that.'

'Happened before. Month back. Same way. Goin' to be hard to get driver and guard next time on.'

Herne sniffed, leaning back in the chair in the Sheriff's office, looking around. Thinking that lawmen's rooms were the same all over. Board with some fly-blown notices pinned crookedly to them. Back door through to the cells. Rack of Winchesters and Meteors, chained together. Desk and a couple of seats. Iron round-bellied stove with some of last winter's ash still cluttering up its base.

And the same kind of lawman.

There were easy towns and hard towns and Herne had known plenty of both. Stow Wells was an easy one. You could tell that by watching Sheriff Clifford V. Williamson.

The most trouble he'd normally get to see would be a couple of cowboys getting themselves drunk and raising some kind of hell with the girls from the Inside Straight across the street.

Williamson had the stamp of a man who'd lived too easy for too long. Now there were hard times poking their noses over the hills around him and he wasn't rightly ready for them.

During the silence Herne stood up and walked to a small table near the barred and shuttered window that opened on the street. Pouring himself a cup of coffee that a rosy-cheeked woman had carried over for them both from the eating-house across the way. It was good coffee, hot and black and strong enough to float a marble clock.

'I heard plenty of you, Herne,' said Williamson, breaking the silence.

'I heard nothing 'bout you,' replied Jed, wiping his lips on his sleeve.

'Heard years back you'd gotten married. And then that you was dead.'

'Part true.'

'Yeah. You surely are kind of a legend.'

'I know it. And it don't do a damned thing for the way I live, Sheriff.'

'Take care of one of our colts here in town.'

'Blackstone.'

'Hell!' The Sheriff couldn't hide his surprise, his boot-heels slipping off the edge of the desk so he nearly fell.

'Seamus Blackstone. Red-headed kid.'

'Now how the . . .? You just rode in here. I know for a fact you can't have been through Stow Wells in the eighteen years and . . .' he paused, calculating on his fingers. 'In the eighteen years and seven months that I've been the law here. So how come you've heard about Seamus?'

'I hear things.'

'Oh, sure.' Williamson continued to look puzzled, but

wasn't prepared to push it. 'You've not been this way before?'

'No. Not through this place in the daylight. Camped close by once.'

'You get to see most places, I guess.'

'Yeah. And they all look just around the same, Sheriff.'

Herne's reputation as a gunman and shootist had ridden well before him. For years now he'd hardly ever met a lawman who hadn't been nervous, seeing his presence in a town as a signal that some general massacre was about to begin.

Sometimes they were correct.

'You was born up in the Sierras, weren't you?'

Herne was surprised at that one. Not many lawmen knew that much about him.

'Yes. Who told you that?'

'I think it was one of the old-timers from the Home. Yeah, it was. Don't recall which one. All them skinny old bastards looks 'bout the same.'

'Who runs that Home?'

'Miss Lily Abernathy. Widow of the old Colonel. Mighty handsome woman. Her daughter, Andreanna, is . . . what do they call . . .? Yeah. The Matron. Matron of the Home. And she's an even more handsome piece of womanhood.'

'How old are they?'

Williamson crinkled his eyes. 'Miss Lily was a whole mile younger than Colonel Abernathy. Used to be somethin' on the stage back East. She'd be around forty. Ladiest lady I ever seen.'

'The daughter?'

'Andreanna's twenty-three next month.'

The speed and accuracy of the reply indicated that Sheriff Clifford V. Williamson might have more than just a passing interest in Miss Andreanna Abernathy.

'How many men there?'

'Twenty, give or take who died this morning. All between sixty and eighty-five. Hardly any of them more

27

than ten cents in the dollar.'

Herne nodded. Though the three he'd met earlier hadn't seemed too far gone.

Williamson reached in a drawer of his desk, fishing out a half-empty bottle of bourbon. Offering it to Herne who silently shook his head. The lawman drew the cork with his teeth and put away a couple of sizable belts of the liquor.

'Better. My Pa always did says he'd never end up in the Home. He died three years back. Your Pa still livin', Herne?'

The instinctive answer was 'No', but the shootist hesitated. It wouldn't have been strictly true.

'I don't know, Williamson.'

'You don't know. Now that's interesting.'

Herne waited for him to go on, but he stayed quiet.

'Yeah,' continued Jed. 'I was born up in the Sierras. February twenty-ninth, 'forty-four. Pa was A.J. Herne, a cartographer with the Frémont expedition.'

'What in hell's a cart . . . whatever you said?'

'Mapmaker. Pa was good. Ma was with him, as they was supposed to be in and out of the high country before the weather broke. Didn't turn out that way.'

'Snow came.'

Herne nodded. 'Yeah. My Ma's name was Elizabeth. Elizabeth Julia Herne. I saw pictures of her. Hair looked blacker than a raven's wings at midnight. That's what my Aunt Rosemary said.'

Williamson took another pull at the bottle. And Herne took some more coffee. Wincing at the pain as the scalding liquid touched on his raw-nerved tooth. Remembering that his next call had to be on the smith. Bisset. Jim Bisset.

'The snows came up on Carson Pass.'

'I been up that way once. Damn it! It was colder'n a well-digger's ass.'

'So Ma had me in a camp. No doctor nor nurse. No other women. I lived and she didn't. Pa took it real hard.

28

Blamed himself for it. When the snows went he took me out East. Had an unmarried sister, Rosemary, in Boston. Big house up on Beacon Hill.'

'She raised you?' asked the Sheriff.

'Tried to. She was powerful fond of French brandy. She was mild and gentle and I walked all over her once I was grown. Left her before I was thirteen.'

'And your father?'

It occurred to Herne that it was a little curious this lawman showing so much interest in his parents, but he was content to talk. Postponing the moment when he had to go and face the blacksmith.

'He left,' he answered, shortly.

'Up and walked?'

'Yes. Vanished into Indian country in the summer of 'forty-four.' He saw the next question already appearing in the lawman's mind and answered it. 'Sure I searched. But he'd gone and that was that. Guess he changed his name. Couldn't live with what happened. Figured maybe that I was kind of to blame as well, just for bein' born. I never saw him again. Never heard a word at all.'

'Nothing?'

'Rumours. I followed out West when I was in my teens. That was when I was riding with Bill Cody out of Fort Bridger with the Pony Express. And I heard a word here and there. Man on his own. Talked a lot to himself. But nothing you could hang a hat on. And that, Sheriff, was that.'

Clifford sniffed, jamming the cork back in the bottle and sliding the remains of his liquor into the desk drawer again. 'That's real interestin', Herne. And now . . . What are your plans? Moving on?'

'I just got here. I aim to move on when I'm ready to move on. Not a whole lot sooner.'

'Your teeth painin' you?' the lawman asked, leaning forward in his chair and staring intently at Herne, as though he'd been studying his face.

'Yeah. I hear the smith'll help.'

29

'Big Jim? Sure will. Gentle as a mother sucklin' her baby. One jerk and all your troubles are over.'

Herne stood up and began to move towards the door when the Sheriff also stood and called across the room.

'Wait on now.'

Herne felt a prickle of tension in the voice and turned slowly. 'What is it, Sheriff?'

'Two things. How old would your Pa be? Supposin' he was still living.'

'Round . . . seventy-two. Seventy-three. That kind of age. Why the damned interest?' The nagging pain from his jaw had shortened Herne's temper to the point where he wasn't likely to suffer fools at all, never mind gladly.

'Nothing. Hold on that rein, Mister Herne. Hold on, there.' The look of anger had frightened Williamson. Red fire had seemed to flare behind the eyes of the shootist and the lawman had felt the chill wind of death brush around the office.

'What else?'

'What?'

'You said there was two things.'

'Sure. If'n you could use a few dollars, it looks like we got us a vacancy as shotgun or driver on the coach, next time it makes a run.'

'When's that?'

'Should be in three days.'

'I can't drive a Concord. Well, I guess I could if'n I had to. Don't have the hands for it. Not the feel.'

'I know someone who'd drive. But not anyone who might ride guard.'

'No. Thanks, Sheriff, but it's not my style.'

'Pay you twenty dollars. Twenty-five.'

'No. Be seeing you.'

He walked out of the cool of the office into the bright sun of late afternoon. There were people on the street watching him and he was sure he caught the movement of someone behind the dusty windows of the saloon. It looked like a man. With red hair.

*   *   *

30

'Igth at on.'

'Sure. I see it, Mister Herne.'

Herne felt the blacksmith touch the tooth that was paining him, sending a white flash of undiluted agony lancing through his jaw. 'Jesus Christ!'

'Guess there's some infection under it. Soon as I draw it that'll start drainin' away. Two or three days and you'll feel great.'

'I'll believe that when I feel it,' replied the shootist.

'Go sit down there,' said the smith, pointing to an old wooden chair in the corner of the forge, away from the glowing fire. 'Hang on that leather strap runnin' under it. Kind of brace yourself.'

The room was unbearably hot and Herne felt sweat coursing down his cheeks, soaking into the collar of his shirt. Running down into the small of his back. At least he figured that it was the heat that was making him perspire so much.

The leather strap was right there and he reached down and gripped it. Fighting the temptation to hang on real tight, forcing himself to relax. Taking several slow, deep breaths. Closing his eyes and easing the tension from arms and legs.

When he opened his eyes again Jim Bisset was right in front of him, blotting out the rectangle of light from the open door. The smith was a big man with broad shoulders and a neatly trimmed beard. His arms and shirt were dotted with scorch marks from the fires and muscles danced beneath the skin.

'You ready now, Mister Herne?'

'Sure. Ready as a stallion facin' the gelding. Get to it, Bisset.'

'There's a cup of water there by your feet. Use it real quick and rinse out when the tooth's gone.'

'Get to it,' repeated the shootist. Opening his mouth, feeling the strong fingers reach in. The taste of smoke on his tongue. A jab of searing pain as the smith's thumb and finger closed shut.

31

Then there was an interruption. A voice from near the door. Young.

'Stand off the stranger, Jim. Leave him be.'

Over the smith's shoulder Herne glimpsed someone holding a gun. And the sun from outside glinted off the boy's bright red hair.

'Shit,' said Jed.

4

'Now, Seamus . . .' began Jim Bisset.

'Shut that flappin' mouth, you stinkin' bag of tripes,' retorted the red-headed stranger. 'And move away slow and easy.'

'Why don't you go play with your toy trains, son,' said Herne, suddenly ice-calm. The tension at having the tooth pulled was totally gone. This was something he knew about now. Something he'd faced before. Might get to face again.

'Don't rile him, Mister,' said the smith, his voice barely a whisper. Outside a wagon rattled by, but inside the forge the three of them seemed locked away in a warm, dark universe.

'Come on Bisset.'

'He's just a stranger, son,' said the big man.

'Don't talk him down for me,' hissed Herne. His temper had finally flared clean over the top and he was angrier than he'd been in long months.

'Hear you call yourself a shootist, old man,' sneered Blackstone, the Peacemaker with its polished barrel and engraved chamber casual in his gloved right hand. Gloves! So many of the kids thought it was smart to wear gloves like the flashy gunmen in the penny magazines they read.

'Go away, boy. Now and for good.'

'You threatenin' me, old-timer?'

'No.'

'Then . . .?'

'A promise, boy. Not a threat. A promise.'

There'd been plenty of times when Jed Herne had been feeling more benevolent, and he'd let kids like Seamus Blackstone walk away alive. But he wasn't in the mood for charity right then, and that was the God's own truth.

'You belong out there with them other crazy old bastards in the Home, you dirty killer. I heard 'bout old men like you. Dirty.'

'Move away, Bisset,' said Herne, quietly, ignoring the tirade from the red-headed boy. Sweat gleaming among the cropped hairs of his blonde beard, the big smith stepped a little to the side so that Herne could see Blackstone more clearly.

'Guess you probably like lifting little girls' dresses and fumblin' at them, you stinking old bastard. You ought to be dead. You ain't no. . . .'

'Enough!!' shouted Herne, powering himself to his feet, hand dropping to his right hip faster than Seamus Blackstone had ever seen anyone move before.

So fast that the boy didn't even believe what he was seeing.

There'd been times before that Seamus Blackstone had crossed paths with strangers in Stow Wells. He had the reputation as being a bit of a no-good boy, eager for a quarrel with anyone that he thought weaker than himself. Three times in the last two years he'd drawn on drifters passing through the small settlement, killing them with a casual ease. The long hours he practised with his hand-gun paying dividends against men with no skill as shootists.

Herne was the sky and the stars better than the boy, long years of killing paying their own dividend for him.

Even as he started to come up from the old chair his right hand was down, flicking the thong off the top of the Colt's hammer. Beginning the draw. He didn't stand upright, holding himself in a low crouch, body slightly turned to the right to make a smaller target.

Blackstone had the chance to fire off a single shot, but

the speed of the middle-aged shootist blurred his mind. He jerked at the trigger, his mouth falling open in a frightened gasp of shock and fear. The pistol bucked in his gloved hand.

Herne was concentrating on killing the red-headed boy and he was barely aware that a shot had been fired at him. There was the booming sound of the gun and a burst of powder-smoke that momentarily obscured Blackstone. The shootist was conscious that the smith had been hit, glimpsing him shudder sideways, clutching at his muscular shoulder and yelping in pain.

But none of that mattered to Herne.

What mattered was his own eye and brain and arm and hand. All combining together with lethal efficiency.

His first shot hit the boy high in the chest, kicking him backwards, the pistol dropping from his suddenly nerveless fingers. Blackstone tried to scream with the thunderous impact of the blow to his body, but the bullet had ripped into his lungs and there was no air to breathe. Blood came to fill his mouth, dribbling down over his chest, pattering among the dry straw in the forge.

Herne's second bullet caught the staggering boy in the face, smashing his nose to shards of splintered bone, the distorted lead angling upwards and sideways, pushing the right eye clean out of its socket so it dangled obscenely on his cheek.

Seamus Blackstone was dying.

He toppled backwards, rolling so that he caught the heavy iron tripod that supported one of the pans of charcoal embers. Spilling the glowing ashes all over himself. His clothes catching fire in a dozen places at once, the smithy filling with the stench of scorching flesh and cloth.

The boy's legs twitched and kicked out as he lay burning, on his back. His hand clutched at the gaping raw socket where his eye had been. His lips parted as though he was going to try and speak but all that came out was pink froth from his ruptured lungs.

'Jesus Christ Almighty!' sighed Jim Bisset, leaning with one hand against the wall of the forge, staring down unbelievingly at the twitching corpse of Seamus Blackstone, red hair puddled with his own blood, matted in the dirt.

'You hurt?' asked Jed, starting to reload the pistol.

'Nicked me in the top of the left arm. Seems to have gone clean on through. Yeah.' Examining the plaster behind him. 'There it is. Figure I'll dig that out and keep it to remind me of this day.'

'Let's have the gun, Herne,' said a voice from the doorway.

The shootist didn't turn around. Didn't need to. 'Hello, Sheriff,' he said. 'Like the damned law the whole country over. Too damned little and too damned late.'

'The pistol,' warned Williamson.

'The kid had already drawn,' said Bisset.

'Bull's chips,' spat Williamson. 'Seamus wasn't that stupid that he'd hold a gun on a man. And then get hisself killed. Just don't seem likely.'

'It happened,' insisted the smith. 'I seen it, Clifford. Kid shot me.'

'Bad?'

'Nope. Flesh wound. I'll get it bandaged up and it'll be good as smilin' in a couple of days.'

Herne finished reloading the pistol, rolling the chamber with the palm of his hand, listening to the soft, whirring click. Holstering the Colt, but leaving the strip of rawhide clear of the hammer.

In case.

'You drew on him and killed him, Herne?'

'You've been told it twice, and already you're startin' to get the picture clear. That's real bright of you, Sheriff.'

Williamson wasn't going to be pushed. His own gun was steady on the shootist's midriff. And Herne knew better than to argue with a cocked double-barrel Meteor ten-gauge. At that range it would have come close to blowing him clean in half.

'We'll take you over the jail for an hour or so, Herne. Get this sorted out.'

'But I already told you. Cliff. We all knew that kid'd get to buy the farm one day. It just happened that Mister Herne here was first in line for it.'

'Shut your mouth, Jim. I'm the law and I do what seems right.'

'Sure,' muttered Bisset. 'But it don't . . .'

'Jim,' warned Williamson.

'Sure. Sure.'

'You don't get my gun, Sheriff. Not just like that. I'll come to the jail with you, of my choosing. I'll tell you what happened. You get the smith to tell you. Anyone else wants a say . . . Fine. Then after that I ride on out of your town.'

Most of Stow Wells had gathered in the doorway of the smithy, whispering to each other in excitement and shock. First the stage, and now young Seamus gunned down by the tall stranger. There'd never been a day like it in living memory.

'I can make you drop the gun.'

'You don't look like a killer to me, Williamson. There's somethin' round the eyes and you don't have it. Some lawmen like it hard. I figure you for someone kind of likes it easier. I'm givin' it you that way. Someone sweep up that garbage,' pointing at the motionless body of the red-head. 'And I'll walk to your jail with you.'

That's the way it was.

There had been a few angry shouts from the citizens of Stow Wells as Sheriff Clifford V. Williamson led Herne across the main street, into the cool of the office. Despite the calling and the protests, the lawman slammed the door closed and slid the bolt across it.

'There. Make sure we don't get interrupted.'

The shootist sat silent, looking at the Sheriff, wondering what he had on his mind.

'Guess you're wonderin' what I have in mind?' asked

Williamson.

Herne shook his head. 'No. Can't say I was. I'm just wonderin' how long you figure on wasting my time here. That's all.'

'About as long as it takes you to agree to ride shotgun in a couple of days.'

'You got a driver?'

'Sure. Old Roy Goddard'll do it. Do anythin' for a couple of bottles of liquor. Used to drive a Butterfield. Got fired for drinkin' on the job. Turned a coach over and killed a couple of nuns. He'll do it.'

Herne grinned. A thin, mirthless smile that brought Williamson up sharp. Blinking and suddenly licking at lips that had gone dry.

'Now, Mister Herne . . . There ain't . . .'

'I'll do it.'

'Well, I . . .'

'Not because of your brainless bastard idea of tryin' to pressure me. That kid was worthless trash and the whole town knows it. I'd back that Jim Bisset to stand up and tell the truth.' There was a pang from his temporarily forgotten tooth. 'Even though he can't draw my rotten tooth for me with that bullet through his arm.'

'It wasn't . . .'

'Fifty dollars.'

'Thirty.'

The shootist smiled again. 'Let's settle at forty-five dollars and call it halfway.'

Williamson couldn't understand it. As soon as he heard the shooting he'd guessed that it was Seamus and the stranger. Yet he hadn't figured on Herne being so damned good. But immediately he'd seen the boy's corpse, he'd seen a chance to blackmail the middle-aged gunman into doing him a big favour.

It had gone wrong.

Now Herne had more or less volunteered for the job of shotgun on the stage, and at a far higher price than Williamson had ever intended paying. And the lawman was only too aware that the shootist had backed him down in front of the whole town.

It hadn't been a good day at all.

That night Herne checked himself into a room at the rear of the Inside Straight, taking up a half bottle of whiskey and a plate piled high with two thick steaks and a mountain of hash brown potatoes. It had been a long, hard day, and the prospect of riding guard in a couple of days' time didn't fill him with excitement. It was a lousy job. Ninety-nine rides out of a hundred it was plain boring.

The hundredth time it was lethal.

Before he undressed and went to bed Herne inched open the warped window, finding that it wouldn't rise more than three or four inches, letting in the cooler air of the Arizona night. From down the stairs he could hear the sound of an out-of-tune piano and the occasional high-pitched yelp of laughter from one of the soiled doves who worked there.

Sheriff Williamson had suggested that maybe the shootist might like to take advantage of one of those 'ladies', on the town, so to speak. But Herne had shaken his head and firmly refused.

'Thanks, Sheriff,' he'd replied. 'There've been times when I've found comfort there, but this isn't one of those times.'

Women were just there to be used. That was Jed's simple creed. And if they didn't like it then he wouldn't waste energy trying to persuade them.

The window from his room looked out across a narrow alley, then a line of outbuildings. And beyond that was the desert. As wild and desolate as it had been for the last thousands of years. Herne thought for a few moments on how weak and shallow was man's grip on the land of the South-West.

His eye was caught by a movement among the shadows between the storage sheds and privies. There was someone hiding and he instinctively wondered whether Seamus Blackstone might have some vengeful relative or friend out there.

There was a full moon sailing serene and untroubled overhead and it gave him sufficient light to make out that the figure was one of the old men from the Home in his uniform of dark blue pants and cream shirts. As soon as he saw Herne peering at him the old-timer scampered away out of sight.

Jed wondered who he was and why he was taking such an interest in his presence in town.

5

Herne slept well.

Over the years he'd learned the skill of slipping easily into an untroubled darkness, yet ready to come instantly awake at the slightest odd sound. There had been a period when he'd been plagued by awful nightmares of his dead wife. Seeing her climbing on a beam in a cold barn, the snow white all around, her breath pluming out and hiding her pretty face. And he had been unable to stop her, his feet seeming to be trapped in thick molasses.

The dream would always end with her falling into space, laughing. Laughing! While he looked up at her, helpless, seeing her drop slowly towards him. Then the sharp snap as the hemp noose jerked tight around her slender neck.

Time had eased away that nightmare for Herne.

During that first morning he walked over to the smithy, to see how Jim Bisset was feeling. He found the big man sitting with his feet up on a bench, the fires dead in the braziers. The blacksmith had his arm tied in a sling, but he was in good spirits.

'Good day to you, Mister Herne,' he called. 'Hear that Clifford talked you into taking the job of shotgun on the next stage.'

'You could say that.' The shootist paused a moment. 'Then again, you could say that I'd agreed that the money was right for it.'

'They'll be layin' Seamus to rest later.'

'Yeah.'

'You'll not go?'

The tooth was still paining Herne. While breaking his fast he'd bitten hard on a boney piece of gristle in the smoked ham and it had jarred his jaw. It hadn't left him in the best of spirits.

'No. I'll not be goin' up the hill. I seen enough buryings to last most men.'

Bisset didn't reply for a while, looking past the tall, lean shadow of the gunfighter, out into the sunlit Arizona street. Coughing and spitting in the straw.

'You figure it's Indians?'

'Tacklin' the stage? Could be. Not like Chiricahua to go for robbery.'

'That Mendez has white blood in him. Well . . . Mex blood, if you can call a greaser white.'

'I don't generally call a Mex anything,' replied Herne. 'Scalping looked like Indians. Whole town seems certain sure it's Mendez and his war party of young bucks.'

Bisset nodded. 'Sure sorry about that trouble with the boy.'

'Not your doin', Bisset. Just damned sore that you never got to draw this rotten tooth of mine.'

'Can't do it with my left hand. But I figure this arm'll be well enough in three . . . four days. Then I'll do it. And not charge you a cent. On the house.'

Herne grinned. 'I'm surely popular. You offer me a free tooth out and the Sheriff offered me a whore. Can't wait for the next offer.'

Drink dulls pain, so Jed bought himself a bottle of whiskey, taking it to his room. The owner of the saloon had heard all about the lethal speed and short temper of the shootist and had offered him the 'best room in the house', in place of the one overlooking the alley. This was a front double with a white-painted balcony, over the street.

There he sat, watching Stow Wells go about its

business and deriving a certain satisfaction in the way everyone knew he was there but nobody would actually look openly up at him. Except for the children and they were swiftly slapped for their temerity.

One of the girls from the sporting-house along the street came to see whether she could interest him in doing some business. When she found that the tall stranger wasn't in the buying vein, she stayed a while to talk with him, sharing the same shot-glass. Giving him an entertaining commentary on the citizens of the small township.

Entertaining and scurrilous.

'See him? Old goat with the little beard and eyeglasses? That's J.W. Locke. Owns the hardware store. Married thirty years come next Thanksgiving. Eleven children born. Eight livin'. Elder of the church meeting society. Member of the council. Mighty big man around Stow Wells is Mister J.W. Locke.'

The laughter as she spoke told the shootist that she knew more about Mister Locke than Mister Locke was likely to want made public. But the liquor had loosed the young whore's tongue.

'Not so big and mighty when he comes around our house. My God but he ain't.'

Herne relaxed in the warm sun, conscious that the pain from his jaw had slipped away a little. Wondering whether, after all, he might not take advantage of the girl's offer.

The whore, who couldn't have been more than fifteen, shuffled her seat closer along the balcony. It was warm and she was only wearing a thin cotton shift with a lace shawl low across the top of her swelling breasts. Herne could almost taste the sweetness of her body. The faint scent of her sweat beginning to rouse him.

'Want to know about Mister Locke?'

Herne nodded.

She laid a hand on his arm, the fingers butterflying their way along the inside of his wrist. Rubbing at the

43

centre of his palm in a small, delicate circle. Smiling up at him and licking her lips in the provocative way that she had learned when she first began whoring four years earlier.

'Let me whisper.' Dropping her voice, her mouth close to his face so that her breath stirred the fine hairs inside his ear. 'Old J.W. gets real excited when I dress up for him. Pretend I'm a little girl at school. Pinafore and knee stockings. No drawers. He comes in like he's the teacher and he has to examine me. See I haven't been . . . you know . . . touchin' myself.'

Herne knew that he was going to lie with this girl.

'Then he says that he intends to give me a good thrashing for my wickedness. Makes it sound like something from the Bible, he does. But he gets off all his fine clothes to tie me up. And I have to ask him if I can tie him first, as I'm kind of frightened by the idea.' She laughed so loudly that a brace of passing housewives walking slowly across the street looked disapprovingly up at the balcony.

'I get him tied tighter than a calf at first branding and he wriggles and struggles. But only kind of pretend. And his pecker gets all hard. Hard as it ever gets with J.W. Locke. I whip him some and then he begs me to let him do dirty things and I let him. Things you wouldn't rightly believe.'

Herne would have believed. He'd once spent three weeks in a Juarez whore-house recovering from a razor-cut to his left wrist. Things he'd seen there were enough to keep his imagination going for the rest of his life. But he was not bothered by what people wanted to do in private. Long as they didn't do it in the street and frighten any passing horses.

The girl was about to go on but she saw the slim figure of the Sheriff strolling by. He stared up at her and she waved a cheeky hand.

'There's Clifford V. Williamson, the Lord bless him! He's kind of cute. Been the law round here for years they say.'

'Honest?' asked Herne.

'Sure is.'

It was the turn of the shootist to laugh. 'I never hardly met a lawman who could say the word "honesty" without crapping in his breeches at the thought.'

'There's Mister Goddard,' she said, suddenly, pointing to a smaller saloon down the street.

'Stage driver?'

'Used to be. Drink sort of fuddled his mind but he's really kind to us girls when he comes on by. Don't see him much now he's lost his job.'

Goddard was short and plump, a salt and pepper beard decorating his chin. Herne watched him, seeing that there was that exaggerated care in walking that comes with the never sober. Not to be confused with the perpetually drunk, who inhabit the next house along the line. The stout figure disappeared through the bat-wing doors of the saloon.

'He likes me . . .' began the girl, but Herne was distracted by the sound of wagon wheels, coming in from the north of Stow Wells at a fair lick.

'Who's . . .?'

'Miss Lily Abernathy. Ain't nobody else drives like that.'

'Lady runs the Home for the old men?'

The whore nodded, leaning forwards to look over the painted rail, towards where a swirling cloud of dust showed the movement of the rig.

'Sure. Her and her daughter. The Matron. Miss Andreanna. Hell of a couple, Herne.' Her hand was off his arm. And down onto his thigh, squeezing with a slow, langorous movement, easing higher and higher.

The shootist was interested. Interested in seeing the two women. And he managed to close his mind for a few moments to the attentions of the girl. Seeing a buckboard come bouncing along the street, stopping outside the dry goods store. There were two women in it. The driver, handling a long carriage whip with the skill of a Tupelo mule-skinner, was in her forties. Tall, in a fur-trimmed jacket of rich blue, and a long skirt in a lighter colour. Her hair was grey-blonde, piled high on her head and held in place with a glittering ruby pin. If the other girl was her daughter, she must be in her twenties, though she looked older. She wore a plain leather jacket over a divided skirt that came only to mid-calf. Beneath it were a pair of gleaming riding-boots with tiny silver spurs.

'You seem mighty interested in them, Herne,' pouted the girl, pinching him to recover his attention for herself.

'Sure. Heard plenty 'bout her since I came to town.'

'She has a lot of power. Most men hereabouts lust after her. Run about with their tongues danglin' for her. For the both of 'em. But none of them ever gets more than a sniff at her.'

'That one of the oldsters in the back of the rig there?'

There was a hunched figure squatting in the bed of the rig. He had a blanket huddled over his scrawny shoulders. His head turned towards the couple on the balcony.

'Yeah.'

'You know them?'

The girl laughed again. Her hand was right at the top of the shootist's leg, fondling his swelling maleness.

'No. All old men look the same, Herne. Blue pants and them white shirts with the big sleeves. All look the same. They come and they go. Some been there years. Some only a day or so. Hear that one died within an hour of gettin' there. Probably saw Miss Lily and that was too much for the poor bastard.'

'She's a mighty handsome woman,' said Herne, quietly.

'Which one?'

'Doesn't much matter, does it?'

Across the narrow street the wagon stayed still, its black, sharp-edged shadow clear beneath it. The figure under the blanket remained motionless, though Herne was sure he could make out eyes flickering like bright gems in the darkness of the makeshift hood.

'Hell-fire and perdition!' exclaimed the young whore.
'What's wrong?'

'Miss Lily just peered out through the store window and maybe saw me up here.'

'She won't be pleased?' he guessed.

'Not likely,' she stammered. Her hand leaving Jed's crotch. She stood up and ducked low, scurrying back inside the bedroom. Her voice floating out from within.

'Us ladies of the night ain't supposed to be seen like this. Out in the open with a gentleman.'

Herne grinned at the alarm in the girl's voice. But it didn't surprise him. He'd seen the effect that upright, God-fearing ladies of a community could have in ridding their towns of women like the young whore. There could be tarring and feathering. And it would be ladies like Miss Abernathy and her daughter that could be at the forefront of such movements.

As he watched them come out of the store and walk slowly along the elevated boardwalk, talking animatedly, Herne wondered what went on behind the neat, tight clothes. Wondered about the dreams that disturbed the long hot nights of the Arizona summer.

'Come on in here,' hissed the girl from the darkness behind him.

The shootist watched the two women until they disappeared into a draper's, pausing to acknowledge Sheriff Williamson as he crossed over the street to tip his hat to them.

The figure in the wagon still didn't move at all, head half-turned.

Watching.

'You comin' in, Mister Herne?'

He was. 'Maybe.'

'Why don't you just come on inside here. Where it's cooler?'

He went inside and joined her.

But it wasn't cooler.

6

The coach was ready a half hour before dawn. The signs of the bloody battle had been cleaned off, but there were still dark stains around the seat and inside the body of the Concord. Herne had been up since five, checking that his horse was well cared-for, stopping off for a word with Jim Bisset.

The sight of the big blacksmith with his shoulder still supported in a sling, brought back the memory of the pain from his rotten tooth. Herne experimentally touched the very tip of his tongue to the tooth. Soft and gentle as a girl with her first lover's gift of a rose.

'Fuck!' he breathed. Eyes squeezing tight, mouth screwing up with the pain. Holding his breath until the lancing spears had moved from his jaw. He sighed, whistling through his pursed lips. Shaking his head at how bad it had been, not surprised to find that his forehead was beaded with sweat.

'Hey, Herne,' called the voice of the law. Clifford V. Williamson, waving a friendly hand towards the shootist. The Sheriff was sharply dressed in black, with a brocade waistcoat decorated with glowing colours of orange and deep green.

'Mornin', Sheriff.'

'Just soberin' up your driver over yonder,' a cocked thumb indicating an eating-house two doors along from the Inside Straight.

'I'll wait.'

'He's on his ninth mug of coffee right now,' grinned

Williamson. 'Hot and black enough to float an anvil.'

Herne breathed, moving his fingers slowly to keep circulation moving. It had been cold earlier and only now was the rising sun giving a pearly glow to the morning.

'There's a scattergun bucketed along the seat there,' said the Sheriff.

'I'll take my Sharps along.'

'Not much use from a moving stage.'

'I can get down, Williamson. And then. . . . If I can see it, then I can hit it.'

'Sure. There's a small load today.' He dropped his voice suddenly and looked around. There was nobody within fifty paces but he kept his voice at a whisper. 'Truth is, there's a pay-load, silver. Worth around seven thousand dollars. Banker's shiftin' it out today. Figures they won't hit twice in three days. Bastard Chiricahua. And that son of a bitch. Mendez!'

'We'll gather at the river . . . the beautiful, beautiful, beautiful fuckin' river. . . . That flows by the throne . . . throne . . .'

Goddard erupted from the eating-house with the speed and violence of a bursting boil. Landing on his backside in the street, managing by a miracle of balance to keep his battered stetson in place. Looking back behind him as he staggered to his feet, making an obscene gesture with his clenched fist.

'By the throne of God . . .' he finished.

'Over here, Roy. Come meet the shotgun we got you,' called the Sheriff.

'Fuckin' shootist, ain't he? Herne. Herne the fuckin' Hunter. Heard of you. Good to have you ridin' with me. Fuckin' good.'

As he shook the leathery hand offered to him the shootist was almost knocked clean off his feet by the man's breath. It was like walking through a blazing liquor store. But the shake was firm enough, the hand strong and steady.

'Good to meet you, pardner,' he said.

'You ridden shotgun 'fore today?'

'Few times. You driven a stage 'fore today?'

Goddard laughed, throwing back his head, showing a mouth filled with three teeth, each of them a masterpiece of decay. 'Few fuckin' times, Herne.'

'You drive fast?'

'I got two speeds, pardner. Fuckin' remarkable and even more fuckin' miraculous. Today you may get to see both.'

'Time you was moving along, now,' said Williamson. 'Should be through to Burned Mill Creek by noon. On to Marks Hill by evening. Back here a little after noon on the morrow. Good luck.'

'No passengers?' asked Herne.

'Hell. I near forgot. Course there is.'

The driver spat on the ground a fraction of an inch from the toes of the lawman's boots. 'More damned trouble than they're worth. Fuckin' passengers.'

'There's only two. Ramrod from the Nolan spread. And Mister J.W. Locke himself.'

Goddard spat again. 'That dumb bastard couldn't find his ass with both hands.'

'Makes more money than you and me'll ever make,' replied Williamson.

'Sure. So did Frank, Jesse, Cole and the rest. Doesn't mean it's right.'

Herne turned away from what was obviously an old and long-standing argument. Climbing up on the driver's box, perched over the oilskin front boot. It was strapped shut and he guessed that the strong-box was already in there. Perched eight feet in the air he looked around the little town. Seeing a group of the oldsters from the Home lurking around the corner of one of the alleys. He recognised Ben and Paddy from two mornings back and gave them a quick wave of the hand as he settled the Sharps rifle between his knees. The two old men looked startled and then both waved back. There was a third man with them, who didn't wave.

Jed checked the Meteor scattergun on his left, making sure it was loaded. Williamson had given him a handful of spare cartridges for it and he felt in his pocket to ensure they were there. Living meant being careful, and that specially meant taking care of your hardware.

The Concord rocked as Goddard clambered alongside him, wheezing like a mule going up a ladder. The driver settled himself down and grinned across at the tall shootist.

'Soon be off.'

Herne didn't reply. It was some time since he'd ridden the box and he didn't feel that much confidence in going with a notorious drunk. To handle four strong horses pulling over a ton of coach at speeds ranging up to thirty miles an hour wasn't easy with the best of drivers. He wasn't certain that Roy Goddard was anywhere close to being the best of drivers.

J.W. Locke appeared suddenly from across the street and walked to the coach, opening the door and climbing in without a word to Herne, the Sheriff or Goddard.

'Morning, Mister Locke. Morning, Mister Goddard. And how are you, Mister Locke? Fine, thank 'e, Mister Goddard,' said the driver, playing both parts with much smiling and tipping of his hat.

A cold voice floated up to them from inside the Concord. 'Guard your tongue, you drunken sot. Or I'll have you whipped from Stow Wells for good.'

Goddard ignored him, winking at Herne. Leaning so far sideways that he nearly toppled off the box. 'Ain't got my head to rights yet,' he slurred. 'Any Jehu can drive a rig blindfold and asleep. If'n he's any good.'

'Meant to ask,' said Williamson, still standing near the pair of bay wheelers. 'How come you drivers get called Jehu?'

It was Herne who answered him. Quoting from the Bible. 'The driving is like unto the driving of Jehu, the son of Nimshi, for verily he doth drive most furiously.'

Goddard cackled. 'Fuckin' truth in the Good Book,

Brother Herne. Fuckin' furiously. Yeah.'

Williamson laughed. Pausing as they heard footsteps coming up from the other side of the main street. 'Hey, Job. Job Burnham, ramrod of the Nolan ranch out of town. Been there six months. Job, this is Jed Herne.'

The foreman was tall as Herne, but at least fifty pounds heavier. Belt hooked under a spreading paunch that was barely concealed by a nice-fitting cotton shirt. He looked around thirty, eyes close-set under bushy brows. His lips were full and red beneath a drooping moustache. Burnham had the kind of face that looked as though it laughed a lot and enjoyed a good time and a glass or two of cool beer at the end of the day and a merry yarn. The kind of man that knew that everyone would like him.

From that first glance Herne disliked him.

From the moment that Roy Goddard cracked the long whip and urged the leaders off Jed Herne's worries about his driver vanished. Despite the toll that drink had taken of his skills, Goddard was still good enough and then some. He tugged on a pair of gloves of the finest doeskin that the shootist had ever seen, even on a woman. Explaining that he had to keep his feel on the ribbons, adjusting the bunches of reins in his hands and clucking his tongue at the team of four horses.

Jed watched the man's skill, seeing how the reins were looped in the left hand, wrapped around the fingers, held loose and easy. Goddard kept his right hand free for the whip and in case he needed the brake, though he'd told Herne that this run was soft and gentle as driving a coach and four across a table-top.

'Been too fuckin' long.'

'What?'

'Too fuckin' long.'

'What has?' Herne found that he needed to raise his voice to a full shout if he wanted to be heard by

Goddard. The pounding of the hooves, the jingling of the harnesses and the rattling of the Concord combining to make conversation exceeding difficult.

'Since I drove.'

'How long?'

Goddard considered the question, transferring a hunk of chewing tobacco from his left cheek to his right. 'Too fuckin' long,' was the final reply.

'Glad to be here?'

'Yeah.'

Herne leaned back, holding on the rail with his left hand, knees pressed together to keep the Sharps rifle safe. If it hadn't been tied down with a leather thong the Meteor scattergun would have long since disappeared over the side of the cascading rig.

Stow Wells was already ten miles behind them. Goddard seemed intent on proving that all his old skill was still there, pushing them on at a good lick. Occasionally urging the lazy nearside wheeler with a scattering of pebbles he carried in his jacket pocket.

'Be early at Burned Mill Creek,' shouted the driver.

'Better five minutes late this world than thirty years too soon in the next,' replied the shootist, grinning sideways at Goddard. Beginning to like the middle-aged drunk. Enjoying the ride, and the fact that he was getting paid for it. The next day he'd be able to ride on from Stow Wells in better shape then he'd entered it.

The rear wheel bounced over a jagged boulder and the whole coach lurched. For a sickening moment Herne thought they were tipping and he grabbed on with both hands. The sudden movement sending a stabbing pain through his jaw.

'Christ!' he yelled.

'Had you worried, Herne!' cackled Goddard, spitting out the mangled tobacco. As it sailed away through the teeming, baking air, Herne had a moment to notice that it looked uncommonly like something you might find on your boots after a walk through a cow-pasture.

'Got a bad tooth. Rattled it.'

'Get Big Jim Bisset to pull it. Son of a bitch pulled all mine.'

'Aim to. When we get back.' By then he guessed that the blacksmith's injured arm should be well enough for him to tug out the offending molar.

He hoped so. It had been going on for entirely too long.

They slowed down some when they reached a rocky defile two-thirds of the way to Burned Mill Creek. The trail wound to and fro among steep-sided arroyos and Herne took his Sharps and held it across his lap.

Goddard saw the movement and grinned crookedly. 'Yeah. I fuckin' figure it too. This is as fuckin' good a place as any if them Indians come a'callin' on us.'

'You figure it for Mendez?' asked the shootist, eyes raking the edges of the cliffs ahead and around them.

'Chiricahua?'

'Folks say it.'

Goddard shook his head. 'I drove more years'n you've had hot dinners, Herne. I never once got me attacked by Apaches.'

'Never?'

'No. Pawnee. Arapaho. Sioux four or five times. Plenty of fuckin' breeds. Never an Apache.'

The shootist nodded his agreement. 'Yeah. Maybe we'll see. Maybe not.'

'I never seen it, that's all.'

The shootist recalled something that his old friend Whitey Coburn used to say. 'You can keep all your yesterdays. They mean nothing. It's just the one tomorrow that's worth thinking on.'

The driver half-turned. 'Ain't that the fuckin' truth, Herne. Ain't it.'

There hadn't been much sign of their two passengers. Once the chilling Mister Locke had rapped on the side of the driver's seat with a silver-topped cane to draw attention to his complaint that there was a lot of dust blowing through the windows of the Concord, despite the leather curtains being buckled down.

Goddard had replied to him, bellowing an answer over his shoulder. 'Best thing I can offer, Sir, is to wait for rain. Damps the dust wonderful, it does.'

There hadn't been any further words from the storekeeper. But the ramrod, Job Burnham, had been continually calling out to Goddard and to Herne. A stream of jokes that had reinforced the opinion of the shootist about the man. Someone as perpetually merry as the cowboy had to be a first-rate pain in the ass.

They were near the end of the maze of linking ravines, still making good time, when Herne happened to glance behind them.

Back along the winding trail.

'We got us some company, Roy,' he shouted, putting his mouth close to the driver's ear so that the passengers wouldn't hear him.

'Indians?'

'Don't make him through the dust. There's one. . . . No, two.'

'Comin' fast?' yelled Goddard, flicking the whip out and nipping the flank of the nearest horse to keep it working with the rest of the team.

'No.'

'That's good.'

Herne sniffed. 'No. Means there's likely more up front.'

'Fuck it. Damn it and fuck it. Fuck, fuck and fuck again.' It was said with a surprising calm, more like a litany in an echoing cathedral.

The shootist hooked the hammer back on the big fifty-calibre rifle. Easing the retaining thong off of the pistol in his belt.

'Shame we aren't carryin' more guns.'

'The ramrod must be able to use a handgun. What

about Locke?'

'His idea of defendin' hisself is to try and scare 'em off with the inside of his fuckin' wallet.'

They came to a sharp bend, the Concord slowing right down to little more than walking pace. Goddard was still cursing quietly under his breath. Suddenly stopping.

'Recall gettin' hit by some fuckin' road agents, eight, maybe ten years back. Near San Antone. Three of 'em. No more than raw kids. Rainin' like the end of the world, it was. Had twenty-one folk that day.'

'How many?'

'Twenty and one, Herne. Nine riding inside and another dozen of us out on top. Weather so bad that nobody was in any mood for bandits. Everyone pulled out and let rip. Tore them kids to pieces. Guess they must have been hit by about fifty bullets each. Should have seen the blood . . . the blood and the mud and rain. Jesus!'

The stagecoach lurched again as they hit a deep rut in the road. But the suspension of the heavy leather thoroughbrace absorbed the worst of the impact.

'There they are,' said Herne. 'Stop here.'

There were five figures, strung out across the trail. Around two hundred paces ahead, where the road ran straight and narrow between sheer walls of red-orange stone.

Goddard threw his weight on the brake, the heavy shoe biting on the rim of the wheel, bringing the rig to a pitching, slewing halt. He called out to the team, quieting them.

Herne brought the Sharps to his shoulder, waiting for the bucking to stop. Looking back over the top of the Concord. Watching for the following men to come into sight through the spiralling pillar of pale dust.

'Yeah. Two of them. Whites. That's seven in all.'

'What do we do, Herne?' asked Goddard.

'Could run them.'

'They'll bring down the horses.'

'Yeah. Stay here and shoot the bowels out of the sons of bitches.'

'All seven?'

'Figure on hitting four or five. Should take some of the fighting heart out of them.'

'What is wrong? Why have we stopped here? Driver! I am speaking to . . . Oh, land of Goshen!!' Mister J.W. Locke had finally looked out of the window of the stage and seen the group of robbers, still sitting their horses and waiting patiently for a move.

'There's five of them out yonder and we figure another fuckin' couple out back of us.'

'What shall we do?'

'You don't do anything, Mister Locke,' replied Herne. 'I'm here for that.'

'They are after my silver.'

'Oh, so it's your silver, is it?' grinned Goddard, slipping another chew of tobacco into his mouth and beginning to bite on it.

'Yes. We must fight for it. You must, Herne. That is why you're hired.'

'I didn't get hired to get killed. There's seven against us.'

'There are three of you.'

The long face of the ramrod appeared out of the next window along. 'Hold on there, good pardner. I'm here for the ride.'

'I'll pay well.'

'How well?'

'Five hundred dollars if we can win through those bandits.'

'Wait on,' exclaimed Herne. 'Best make that five hundred each.'

Locke tightened his thin lips. 'You and the driver have contracts. I will not interfere in your conditions of employ.'

'Then I won't interfere with saving your money. Coming, Goddard?'

The driver nodded his agreement, starting to loop the

ribbons around the handle of the brake. A nerve began to tic at the corner of Locke's eye as anger snatched him.

'You can't . . . You are a bastard, Mister Herne.'

'No, Locke. Not true. Might not have seen my Pa for forty years, but he was there when it mattered. And with most bastards it's just an accident of birth. But you, Locke, are really a self-made man.'

'I'll pay you both. Fifteen hundred dollars in all if we can get free.'

Herne nodded. 'Then we'd best set to it. Those five out there won't wait all day. They can just sit there, figurin' us for sittin' targets. They know they've got men behind if'n we try and break and turn and run back to Stow Wells. I'll see what I can do with the Sharps here to slow them down some.'

Behind him he heard the click of the ramrod cocking his pistol. The shootist didn't even look round. 'Won't need that yet, Burnham.'

The ranch foreman's voice was quiet in the sudden stillness. 'Wrong, Herne. I need it right now. Drop the rifle and sit real patient.'

7

'You scum.'

'Sure, Mister Locke. Guess you might think that. But me and my friends think different.'

'How long have you been doing this?' asked Herne, intent on keeping the cowboy talking. From where Burnham leaned from the window of the Concord he couldn't see Jed all that well. And that was an angle worth concentrating on.

'Not long. Easy money.'

'Blame it on Mendez and the Chiricahua?'

Burnham laughed. 'Yeah. Now drop the gun, Herne. I aim to call my pardners over once the buffalo gun's hit the dirt.'

'How come you're here?' asked Goddard. 'You weren't on the other stages that gotten hit.'

'No. They didn't have Mister Herne the Hunter riding shotgun, did they? I'm just here as a kind of insurance. Figured I'd be needed. I was right. Now, Herne. The long gun. In the dirt. Now!'

'Do as he says,' quavered Locke.

'So he'll spare us all?' mocked Roy Goddard, glancing sideways at Herne, trying to second-guess whatever plan the shootist might have.

'They might.'

'Ask him,' suggested Herne.

'The gun, Mister,' warned Burnham, leaning further out of the window to give himself a clearer view of Herne.

'Down there?' pointing to a patch of soft sand among the boulders.

'Fuckin' anywhere.'

'Right.'

'Now, you son-of-a-bitch. I don't give a damn 'bout whether you get it now or later.'

'Sure,' said the shootist, standing and hefting the big fifty-calibre rifle. Heaving it over the right side of the coach, where Burnham could see it.

And diving off the other side.

Snatching up the Meteor as he did so, thumbing back the hammers before he even hit the ground. Rolling off one shoulder and coming up in a crouch, the heavy shotgun braced against his hip.

Burnham's head appeared through the window of the coach, his pistol raking the air, searching for Herne.

Seeing him.

Seeing the scattergun pointed right at him.

Mouth opening in what might have been the beginning of a scream. Or a curse.

Or a prayer.

It didn't much matter.

Herne tugged back on both triggers, feeling the gun kick against him, nearly knocking him clean off balance. A burst of smoke from both barrels and the man in the coach disappearing from sight as utterly as if he'd never existed.

Rising behind the noise of the scattergun was an odd squealing sound. As though someone had buried a butcher's knife in the flank of a prime sow.

Herne dropped the shotgun, starting to move away around the front of the horses, ignoring the sound. He knew that he'd hit Burnham, so the sound wasn't going to be anything important. The team was bucking and rearing, Goddard standing up on the box, fighting them, holding the reins in both gloved hands.

'They're comin', Jed,' he yelled. 'Front . . . front and back.'

The shootist was concentrating on getting to the Sharps rifle. Knowing that if he was fast enough at powering himself to pick up the heavy rifle he should have time to pick away some of the attackers.

The screaming still flowed on.

The Sharps was where he'd thrown it, flat on its side. Herne had taken care not to drop it muzzle down, so that it risked getting blocked and jamming. Out of the corner of his eye he noticed the cloud of dust as the bandits started to come in at the gallop. The boom of the scattergun telling them that things had gone wrong.

'Ones behind are closer!' called Goddard and Herne waved an acknowledgement.

Picking up the Sharps. The familiar weight and balance to the rifle. Flicking back the side hammer and running to the rear of the Concord. Goddard had fought the team and won, holding them steady. As he went past the right side of the coach Herne saw what remained of Job Burnham dangling bloodily from the half-open door. The head had been blasted to shards of splintering bone, the top of the scalp flapping loose as though an Apache had been interrupted at taking the hair. The features were gone, and one arm hung on the shoulder by scraps of gristle.

The noise continued from inside and Herne was now able to place it as being the voice of J.W. Locke. Crouched on the floor of the coach, keening his terror at the way death had blasted from the Arizona morning. Splattering him with brains and gobbets of torn flesh.

Two riders. Closing fast. The nearest whipping furiously at a big grey, less than a hundred paces off.

Jed steadied himself, calming his breathing. Quickly putting a dab of spittle on the sharp foresight from habit. But eighty yards to the fifty-calibre buffalo gun was like shooting at blackboard across a classroom.

Aim, stock firm against the right shoulder. Cheek cradling against the warm wood. Both eyes open, peering along the smooth barrel. Finger tightening . . .

Tightening . . .

'Got the fuckin' whore!' yelped Goddard, waving his hat around in excitement.

The bullet took the rider through the upper chest. A

safer killing shot at a man galloping towards you than going for the skull. This way you had a spare margin all around. Bullet high and it hits him in the head. Low and it rips the guts from him.

The impact of the big slug was enough to pluck the robber clean out of his saddle, leaving him dying in the dirt. There had been no warning. Through the dust he hadn't even noticed Herne at the corner of the stage. By the time his eyes registered that there had been a puff of powdersmoke it was way too late. He was flat on his back looking up at the sun through misting eyes.

By then Jed had ejected the warm brass case, hearing it tinkle among the pebbles by his feet. Taken another cartridge from his jacket pocket and thumbed it into the rifle. Sighting and firing in a single fluid movement that was his inheritance for the long, painful years of practice.

But the man's horse had swerved, pulling away to avoid trampling on the fallen rider, putting Jed off his aim for that vital moment.

'Missed him,' shouted Goddard.

'Start turning the team and shut up!' yelled Herne, knowing instinctively that his second shot had missed. It was still booming out across the roasted land when he fired a third time. This time making no mistake.

The bullet hitting the second of the trailing men in the centre of the throat, angling sideways after it hit the cervical vertebrae of his spine, snapping his neck like a dry twig underfoot. The distorted ball ripped out through the side of his neck, taking the big carotid artery with it. Sending the bandit spinning to the dirt in a wheeling fountain of bright blood.

The pounding of hooves from the other five bandits was getting closer. Goddard had begun the slow process of turning the Concord from a standstill, using his whip on the leaders and cursing them. The cries of distress from inside the coach had gradually faded away to a miserable whimpering.

'Ain't goin' to fuckin' make it, Jed,' shouted the driver. 'Not time.'

'Then hold 'em there. Side on.'

Herne shuffled quickly around to the further angle of the coach, steadying himself and firing twice in quick succession. Lips peeling back from his teeth like a cornered wolf with the satisfaction of seeing two men fall. One horse also went down and stayed down, shot through the side of the head, its legs stiff and kicking. The rider struggled to his feet and called something out to the three survivors.

Who heeded the cry of warning, reining in with a brutal violence, wheeling their animals around and heading off the main trail towards a side canyon. The bandit on foot started to sprint after them. Head back, arms pumping as if he was running a foot race.

Which he was, competing with the speed and accuracy of Herne's shooting.

Herne won.

The bandit lost.

Goddard couldn't stop talking about it. Knotting the ribbons around the brake, locking it on. Jumping down and pumping Jed's hand as though he'd just been elected to the United States Senate by an overwhelming majority.

'Fuckin' amazing.'

'Guess they'll not come after us. Unless they try an ambush.'

But the driver's ears weren't hearing him. He was still locked into the devastatingly lethal display that he'd just seen from the shootist.

'Killed 'em. Fuckin' killed 'em. Like that. Easy as fallin' off a fuckin' bridge. One. Two.' Sighting an imaginary rifle. 'Boom. Three down. Boom. That's fuckin' four. And the others ran like scared fuckin' coyotes with their asses drippin'.'

'Roy,' interrrupted Herne, patiently reloading the rifle. Also ejecting the spent cases from the Meteor and recharging it. 'They might take us if'n we go on. I figure we should head back to Stow Wells.'

'Maybe. Maybe so.'

'Best tell that jelly in there.'

'Hey, if Job Burnham was one of 'em, and you fuckin' blew his head all over my rig, then his five hundred comes to us. Don't it?'

'Should. Seven hundred and fifty of the best for each of us.'

'That right?' called the driver. 'That right, Mister Locke?'

A face whiter than the most spotless bridal veil appeared at the window of the blood-speckled Concord. Eyes blinking furiously, tears still glistening on the merchant's pallid cheeks.

Goddard repeated the question. 'I was askin' whether we'd get that fuckin' money?'

'Money?'

'Sure. You promised us fifteen hundred dollars between us for saving your silver,' said Herne.

'Yes. Yes, I did. Have they gone?'

'Those livin' have gone.'

'Will they come back?'

'Don't rightly know. Be a surprise if'n they do. Mister Herne here sure took a fuckin' toll among 'em.'

'Then let us go.'

'We are.'

'Why are we turning, driver?'

'Goin' back.'

'Where? To Stow Wells?'

Goddard nodded. 'That's about right. No way of knowin' if'n there ain't more of them bastards up yonder. Go on back and maybe make the run in a couple of days with a guard or two out-ridin'.'

'Oh, very well. But I would greatly appreciate it if one of you would remove this . . . this carcass from in here.'

Herne looked across at Roy Goddard. 'Hell, I'll do it, Jed. This team's goin' to be real tuckered out if we don't make a change.'

'I'll get that stray horse,' suggested the shootist. 'Ride

64

ahead to the town and warn them you're coming in. Williamson can arrange an escort for you.'

'Sure. Damn! White men.'

'Yeah. Easier to blame Indians, huh? Still kind of strange that scalping and all on the other trip. Not like. . . . Hell, I don't know.'

He walked out and called in one of the dead bandit's horses, whistling it to him. It was a fine bay mare and it nuzzled against him, standing still as he stroked it, blowing up its nostrils in the way he'd learned from the Oglala Sioux.

He heard Locke moaning behind him about the mutilated corpse of Burnham, drooped half out of the one window. As Herne looked round he saw that Goddard was struggling to heave the body out of the way, totally unhelped by Locke.

'Always said he was a mite impulsive, old Job here,' cackled the driver.

'Impulsive?' shouted Herne.

'Sure. Now he's nearly lost his fuckin' head. Get the joke, Mister Locke?'

But Mister Locke was too busy throwing up on his hands and knees on the far side of the coach.

Five minutes later everything was organised. The body was stretched out in the hot sand. Goddard was back up on the box of the coach, ribbons ready in his gloved left hand. Whip gripped in his right fist ready to start the team. Mister J.W. Locke was half-sitting, half-lying on one of the seats, weeping uncontrollably, deep in shock. But he'd agreed between sobs that Herne and Roy Goddard should share the fifteen hundred dollars equally, soon as they were back in Stow Wells again.

'I'll get the drinks on the bar ready for you,' called Herne, setting heels to the mare, giving a wave to the whiskered driver – a man that he'd come to like during the few short hours he'd known him.

It was the last time that he was to see either Locke or Goddard.

Alive.

8

On the way back into town Herne had checked over the
Sharps. The one miss didn't bother him too much, but the
gun hadn't felt quite right to him. There was something
wrong; but he couldn't put his finger on it. The Sharps
had been with him for so long that it was like an extension
of his body. It was as though a pianist was suffering from
some exceedingly minor complaint, like a hang-nail. But it
would be enough to put him off the finest edge of his
technique.

Though he looked closely at his beloved fifty-calibre
rifle the shootist couldn't actually see anything out of line.
But he suspected that when he'd thrown it down in the
sand it might have struck a hidden stone in the dirt. And
that had been sufficient to jar the gun. When he got back to
Stow Wells he'd take it out behind the houses and test-fire
it. Maybe go to Big Jim Bisset if any work needed doing.

Herne was also his own gunsmith and would rather trust
his own eye and hand against anyone else.

It was a good way of keeping living.

Sheriff Clifford V. Williamson came running from his
office, brought out by a street urchin who'd raised the
settlement with the news that the tall shootist who'd gone
out as shotgun on the morning stage was coming in alone
on a strange bay mare.

'What happened? Jed! Jesus, where's the coach?'

'Out yonder. Take it easy, Sheriff. Don't go get your
breeches filled.'

'You get hit?'

'Yeah. Whites. Seven. Job Burnham was one of 'em.'

'What happened?' Williamson was half-running alongside the shootist, face turned up, surrounded by better than half the settlement.

Herne reined in and swung from the saddle, feeling the sudden tiredness that often came long after violent action was finished and done.

'Job got his head blown apart with the Meteor. I brought down four of the rest with this,' hefting the Sharps. 'Locke is fine. Though I guess he could use a private cleaning-up when he gets back. Goddard's fine. Fine. Good man, that.'

'The silver?' asked someone in the crowd.

'That's safe.'

'Why did you. . . .?' began Williamson.

'Come back?' completed Herne. 'Horses were tired and we figured safest was to turn 'em back here. Do the run again in a couple of days. Guess the Concord should be here in around an hour. Hour and a half.'

'Jesus Christ,' breathed Williamson. 'You sure went out and did it, then. Killed. . . .' calculating rapidly. 'Killed five bandits. All on your own.'

'Locke promised me and Goddard fifteen hundred dollars for savin' his ass and his money,' said Herne. There was no harm in sowing those particular seeds to make it harder for the merchant to go back on his word when he was safe and snug back in town.

Bisset appeared at the edge of the throng. Herne noticed that his arm was already out of its sling and the big man was grinning. Waving the injured hand at the shootist.

'It's a heap better, Mister Herne. If'n you want that tooth pulled?'

Jed shook his head. 'Bath first, thanks. Then some food. Shot of whiskey. And then you can pull the little bastard for me.'

The truth was that the excitement had temporarily

driven away the pain of his tooth. But he knew from experience that it would return. It was good to feel that the killing was over for a while. That he'd earned himself seven hundred and fifty dollars without getting even a scratch. And that tomorrow he'd ride on from Stow Wells without the nagging pain in his jaw.

'Even the losers get lucky some time,' he said to himself as he walked towards the saloon. Wondering as he said it where he'd caught the expression recently. Hearing a call from the balcony and looking up to see the young whore waving to him.

'Lucky,' he repeated, starting to smile. It looked like it was going to be a real good day.

It wasn't.

The water was deep and hot and the girl compliant and enthusiastic. Responding to him, helping him wash. Sitting down to a meal with him, and then joining him in bed again for a half hour after.

They were still in bed when there was the jingle of spurs in the corridor outside the room and the soft sound of someone rapping on the door. Herne reached across the girl, taking the Colt from the holster at the head of the bed. Cocking it and readying it in his fist.

'Who's there?'

'Me. Williamson.'

'Come in, Sheriff,' easing down the hammer. The girl pulling the sheet up over her budding breasts, sliding down the bed, almost out of sight.

The door opened and the lawman stuck his head into the room. 'Sorry to interrupt you, Mister Herne.'

'What?'

'The coach.'

'Holy Jesus!' The shootist had been relaxing and had regarded his job as finished. It had not occurred to him that the coach should have arrived in town. Even allowing for Roy Goddard taking it easy the Concord should have been in Stow Wells at least a half hour back.

'I just. . . .'

But the shootist was already out of bed, starting to get dressed. The whore sat up and made a rude gesture at the Sheriff. 'You just spoiled one of my best times, you miserable bastard, Cliff.'

'Now, Louanne. . . . Can't talk to the law like that.'

'I can talk any way I want.'

'I'll have to get hard with you.'

The girl sniggered. 'Be a change if'n you got it hard for me, Cliff.'

'Now that ain't . . .' began the Sheriff, stopping when he saw the girl's malicious grin. 'I'll tan your hide for you, you. . . .'

'Promises are fine things, Clifford V. Williamson. I'd be mighty pleased to see some action.'

Herne was dressed, ignoring the banter between the whore and the lawman. 'Let's go.'

'Where, Mister Herne?'

'Find the coach.'

'But we. . . .' Williamson stopped when he realised that the shootist had gone.

It was four and a half miles out from Stow Wells.

By the time that the hastily grouped posse of good men and true from the settlement reached it the sun was already sinking far away to the west, dipping beyond the nearest range of jagged mountains. The shadows were long across the desert, thrown behind the men and the horses. Herne had first seen the circling black shapes, etched deep against the darkening sky. Reining in and pointing. The others stopping around him.

'God *damn*!' said Williamson, taking his hat off and nearly throwing it to the earth in his anger.

'Looks like someone got there first,' said Herne, voice calm as a Sunday church social.

'You said there was but three of them bandits left alive?' said one of the shop-keepers. Looking across at

69

Herne as though he was a nasty red figure that had crawled in among the black at the bottom page of an annual balance sheet.

'Yeah. It wasn't them.'

'You sure?'

'One more sneer and I'll push the muzzle of this Colt down your damned throat and pull the trigger,' said the shootist, voice still and unflurried.

'I don't . . .'

'No. That's right. You don't.'

The shop-keeper turned to the Sheriff for support, but he was gazing studiedly out across the desert towards the circling buzzards. The man looked back at the stranger, seeing the tightness around the eyes and mouth. And decided that it might be a good time for keeping quiet.

'You figure it for Indians?' asked Jim Bisset, sitting astride one of the biggest geldings that Herne had ever seen. Its back looked broad enough to support the foundations of a cathedral.

Herne sighed. 'Guess so. Looks like there's traces of smoke. Hard to make it out. Know when we get there.'

'Yeah. Chiricahua. Whole thing makes a kind of sense now. Mendez has scouts out. Each time they see this gang of outlaws after a stage he sits and waits. Comes in to pick up any pieces left around. Little scalping for his young men.'

'Think Goddard and Mister Locke are dead?' called someone from the back of the posse.

'Don't think it. I know it. Less'n they've taken them with them for some sportin'. That could happen. But that makes them good as dead.'

'How many Indians, d'you figure?' asked Williamson, shading his eyes with his hand and looking to where they suspected the coach had met its final end.

'Maybe tell you when I get right there,' replied Herne. 'No point talkin' now. Let's see.'

*   *   *

The shootist wasn't certain about the numbers of the attackers, but he was inclined to think that there might only have been two or three.

The Concord had been stopped in a narrow defile, just before the trail opened to its long wide run into the township. It was burned out clear to the axles. The two lead horses were dead in their traces and the wheelers had disappeared. Arrows clustered in the chests of the dead animals. Unmistakably Apache arrows.

Roy Goddard was lying still and dead a hundred paces away from the charred wreck. The Indians were never kind to the corpses of their defeated enemies and it was hard to tell how he'd met his death. But Herne found the stump of an arrow protruding from the side of his neck and another below the right arm.

'Jesus,' said one of the posse, turning away. 'Why do . . .?'

'Enemy goes on for ever, son,' said Herne, straightening with a sigh. Feeling a twinge of rumbling pain from his rotten tooth. 'So they make sure that old Roy here won't cause no trouble to them in the lands beyond this one.'

The Apaches had done their work well. The scalp had gone, peeled neatly away from the raw top of the skull. The eyes had been gouged from their sockets. Teeth – what had remained of them – battered from the driver's jaw. Ears sliced off and nose slit. Every finger and toe broken. Arms and legs dislocated. The genitals cut off and the stomach opened, intestines draped across the front of the body as it lay, a poor broken thing, on its back in the evening light.

There was no sign of Mister J.W. Locke.

Herne realised that Locke was an important man around Stow Wells. Maybe not as highly regarded as Miss Lily Abernathy and her daughter, but a man of some importance.

Important enough for Sheriff Clifford V. Williamson to order an immediate return to town.

'Then we get food and water for three days and head off after these butcherin' bastards. What do you say, men?'

There was a somewhat grudging cheer of approval.

'You with us, Mister Herne?' asked the blacksmith.

The shootist shook his head. 'Not me.'

'Figured it might be worth it, seeing as how he owes you seven hundred dollars,' said the lawman, unable to keep the anger from his voice.

'Fifteen hundred, seein' poor Goddard's gone and bought the farm here,' replied Herne.

'Then why not come? You surely aren't scared, I know that.'

'I hope you do, Williamson,' snapped Herne. 'Because I can teach you real easy.'

'Then why not?'

'Why?'

'I don't get it.'

'The man's dead, Sheriff,' said Herne, trying to explain in slow, patient tones, as if he was dealing with an idiot child. 'Dead or as good as. Those Apaches have a start on you of . . . maybe two hours or more. By the time you get near them it'll be dark. Maybe you'll lose more men at night. They can circle.'

'Mendez has a big party. Word was he might have thirty warriors.'

'Then this wasn't his main group. Makes it more important you don't go off like your breeches caught fire. Keep patient, Williamson. You'll get to live a whole lot longer.'

'I'll go where I damned well want and do what I damned well want, Herne. You want to go on back to the safety of town and skulk around gettin' sucked dry by that little whore, Louanne. Waitin' for all that money.'

'Locke's dead, you dumb bastard. And my money's dead with him. I'll go back to town right enough. And I'll be long gone 'fore you get back from chasin' after all them wild geese.' There was a murmur of anger, but the

72

shootist wasn't finished. 'Those of you that get back, that is.'

It was only as he rode slowly back along the main street of Stow Wells through the gloom of evening that Herne realised virtually every male between fifteen and fifty-five had gone on the posse.

It would be bad news if Mendez chose to come calling.

9

Louanne was waiting for him, sitting disconsolately at a table in the empty saloon. With no customers most of the local girls had gathered to play a noisy game of penny-ante stud in the corner near the bar. And a couple of Miss Abernathy's oldsters were also in there, one of them quietly picking a tune out of the battered piano by the staircase. As soon as they saw Herne walk in the old men exchanged glances and rose to their feet. Hurrying out of the Inside Straight without a backwards glance at the shootist.

The posse had left earlier, all fed and watered, loaded with extra ammunition and guns. Rifles, pistols and scatterguns. Ready to teach 'that bastard Mendez a damned lesson'.

Herne would be surprised if the posse got close enough to fire a shot in anger at the Chiricahua leader.

There seemed a resentment against the shootist, most of the girls turning away from him, refusing him even the minimal courtesy of a whore's smile. Louanne explained to him that the Sheriff had told folks in Stow Wells that Herne wasn't prepared to ride out with them after the killers of Roy Goddard and the kidnappers of the respected Mister J.W. Locke.

'And some of the girls says you're scared.'

'You say that?' asked Jed.

'No. No, I don't. I just . . . I just figure you must have your own reasons.'

'Yeah.' The shootist saw no reason to explain to a

teenage prostitute how his thinking went. She wasn't important enough for that. She was only really important to Herne for one thing.

And as soon as he'd eaten a quick meal and downed a couple of shots of liquor Herne took Louanne up the broad stairs, past the ornamented golden cherubs at the top, into his room. And used her for what she was best at.

'What time is it?'

'Round five.'

The girl yawned, rolling over on her face, burying her head in her arms. The sheet slipped away from her, revealing her naked from top to toe. Herne glanced once across at her, the sight of her dimpled bottom giving him a brief smile at the memory of parts of the previous night. Then he turned away to something that interested him far more.

'What are you doin'?'

'Cleaning my guns. The Colt and the Sharps.'

'Why?'

It was a question of such staggering stupidity that the shootist didn't even bother to reply.

'They dirty? They sure look clean to me.' She was sitting half up, her breasts red and marked around the nipples with finger-marks where Jed hadn't been too considerate in his handling.

'Fire a gun and it's fouled,' he grunted. Concentrating on his work.

'You didn't use that handgun.'

'There's the fouling from powder. Lead. Dust. Damp. All of 'em work against a gun.'

He'd already cleaned off the sides and the front of the cylinder, using an oiled rag. Barrel and the frame recesses had been wiped clear. He'd cocked both pistol and rifle several times, listening intently to the sound of the actions. Eyes screwed up with the effort of listening, trying to catch the slightest sound of something not quite right. But both guns seemed all right to him.

Herne had also pulled through both barrels to wipe away any lead and trail dirt, wondering whether it might be time for each of his guns to be totally stripped down and boiled and then greased again. Deciding that it could wait another week or so.

'You movin' on?'

'Yeah.'

'When?' No answer. She tried again. 'When? Today? Tomorrow?'

'Probably after noon.'

'Ooh, I'll miss you, Jedediah.'

'Sure you will,' he said, not bothering to conceal his disbelief.

'Truly.'

'Sure.'

She banged one fist on the bed. 'I mean it, damn your lousy. . . .! I mean it, Jedediah. I'll truly miss you when you go.'

He turned and smiled at her. 'Maybe you will at that, girl. But there'll be another drifter along tomorrow. And another on the day after. And on and on.'

'I'd surely like to get out of this.'

'All whores say that, Louanne.'

'Some make it,' she protested.

'Most don't. Drink or a knife. Mainly the former. That's the marker at the end of the line for girls like you. Way it always was. Way I figure it always will be.'

'Maybe I'm different.'

He nodded. 'Maybe you are.'

'I'll show you.'

'Be pleased at that.' Holstering the pistol. Laying the Sharps carefully on the table. Then picking it up again and sighting along the smooth barrel.

'Something wrong with that gun?' she asked.

'Could be.'

'What are you goin' to do?'

'Go out back a quarter mile and try and sight it in again.'

'Shoot?'

'Yeah. Shoot.'

'Can I come?'

Herne sighed. 'Persistent little bitch, aren't you, Louanne? I guess so.'

'Thanks a . . .'

'But you keep out of my way and you keep quiet. And you can mark targets for me.'

'How do I do that?'

'I'll tell you. Now. Get dressed. I'll meet you out the back of the saloon in three minutes from now.'

She grinned at him. And for a moment he remembered Becky Yates, seeing something in the face that was both different yet oddly similar. He hadn't thought of Rebecca for some time and the memory was oddly painful.*

'Three minutes?'

'Yeah.'

The whore jumped out of bed, pink and naked, cupping her young breasts with both hands in a cheeky gesture at the middle-aged gunfighter. 'Be ready in two if'n you don't mind me with no drawers.'

'I don't mind.'

'Then let's to it.'

It was a wonderful morning.

The sun high and serene, swinging imperceptibly across a deep blue sky. The temperature was in the nineties, but a cooling wind kept it tolerably comfortable. As Herne stepped out of the front of the building he blinked, eyes rapidly adjusting to the change in light. It was so clear that he could make out the distant peaks, shimmering through the heat, maybe forty miles away or more. It was odd to walk on a main street of a township like Stow Wells and see it almost deserted.

*For the details of Jed Herne's relationship with the teenage girl see the earlier volumes in the series.

There were a couple of women standing chatting on the corner, along by the deserted forge. As soon as they saw the shootist they deliberately turned their backs on him.

Sitting in a row, like carved ornaments, Jed saw five of the old men from the Home, all in identical wooden chairs, leaning back in the shade of the porch. Five wrinkled heads on scrawny necks turning to watch him move. Five pairs of hooded eyes, like sun-warmed lizards, staring in his direction.

It was an eerie sight.

They walked for nearly a half mile, out towards the neat walls of the Colonel Roderick Abernathy Home For Distressed Gentlemen. Herne carrying the long rifle at the trail, moving fast and light. The girl hobbling after him in absurdly high-heeled calf-length boots, their gleaming black leather quickly dulled by the reddish dust of the desert. She cursed and moaned as she teetered after the tall shootist, holding her skirt up with one hand, to keep it from dragging in the dirt.

'How much further?'

'Guess this'll do. You see that arroyo over yonder?'

'One with the saguaro cactus at its mouth?'

'Yeah. I'm goin' to shoot at that cactus. You hold up one hand for a clean hit. Both for a miss. Got that clear?'

'Sure. One a hit. Two a miss.'

'Right. And after the first hit I want you to point out exactly where it is. Use a stick or something. After that I'll aim to get as close as I can to it. So show me with your hands whether I'm high or low. Left or to the right. Understand that?'

Her face was blank with boredom. Sweat clouded her upper lip and her mouth was set in tight line.

'I asked if you understood, girl?'

'Yeah. Sure I do. It's easy enough. Jesus Christ on the Cross!! It's damned hot out here.'

'This'll take less than an hour. Then we can go back and I'll buy you a drink.'

'And make love again. Before you leave town.'

The shootist nodded. 'Yeah. That too.'

She smiled suddenly. Radiantly. 'You're the best I ever had, dearest Jed. The best that I ever had.'

Then she went hobbling off to where he'd told her, turning a half dozen times to wave to him. Each time he returned the wave. Each time wishing she'd hurry up so that he could get on.

As he waited, cradling the Sharps in his arms, Herne found himself probing with his tongue at the rotten tooth. Hissing at the sudden shock of pain from it. Despite the long days that he'd been suffering with it he still vaguely hoped that it would, somehow, go away. Even though all logic and common-sense told him that it was utterly impossible.

It had gone too far.

A quarter mile or so to his left, north of Stow Wells, the shootist saw a trail of dust winding skywards as a buggy moved fast towards the rectangular building that was the Home. He wondered which of the two women was driving it.

And he wondered again about the strange old man who seemed so interested in him.

Louanne was where he wanted her. Waving a scrap of white material. Herne lifted the rifle above his head as a sign that he saw her and that he was ready to begin shooting.

In his involvement his awareness of the bad tooth slipped away. When Jed Herne did something he did it with all of his energy and attention. Concentrating on calming his breathing. The stock of the buffalo rifle tight against his right shoulder. Dab of spittle on the sight. Both eyes. Bringing the gun steady on the dark jagged shape of the giant cactus.

'One hand.'

A hit.

Watching intently to try and make out where the

whore was pointing. The kerchief a tiny dot. The bullet had hit a little high and right of where he'd thought.

He sighted in and fired again, not altering the gun at all.

'Hit. To the right and high. What I figured.'

The jolt as he'd dropped the Sharps from the stage had jarred the gun. Not enough to damage it seriously, but enough to bring it a little out of line.

He fired ten more rounds, still leaving the sights on the fifty-calibre rifle untouched. There was no point in fiddling with them. All he wanted was a consistent guide to how the gun was firing.

'High and right again,' he muttered after the twelfth bullet. Seeing the figure in the long dress pointing where he'd hit.

In between rounds Louanne was moving away to the side, sitting and resting on a large boulder close to the narrow mouth of the arroyo.

'Try one more,' the shootist said to himself, ejecting the cartridge case, hearing it tinkle to the earth among some small pebbles. Reloading, and tugging back on the hammer.

Looking up. Along the barrel. Holding his breath again.

Easing his finger away from the trigger.

Lowering the gun.

'Where the Hell?'

Louanne had disappeared. One moment she'd been sitting down in clear sight. Now she'd vanished. She'd been complaining about the heat and it crossed Herne's mind that she could have fainted. Or maybe she'd been taken short and retired discreetly behind the rocks, or into the shadowed opening to the ravine.

Maybe.

Jed half-lifted the rifle to his shoulder again, then changed his mind. If she wasn't there to mark it for him, then it was just a waste of time and a bullet to fire it off.

'Damned little. . . .' he said, thumbing the hammer

back down on the gun. Starting off towards the cactus at a brisk walk. Feeling the heat of the sun as it bounced back into his face from the shattered stones all around. He noticed that there were several signs of rattlesnakes in among the mesquite. Sinuous winding trails in soft sand. But he was wearing boots and he knew that it was rare that a snake would deliberately attack a man.

Rare, but not unknown.

When he was a hundred yards off from the ravine he stopped.

'Hey! Louanne! You all right?'

The desert was still, only the whispering of the wind reaching his ears.

'Louanne! You hear me?'

His voice would certainly have carried if she'd been out of sight inside the arroyo. So his first guess was probably correct. She'd likely passed out from the warmth of the day.

Before going into the cool deeps of the sheer-sided ravine the shootist stopped to check out the torn and pulped cactus. Raising a hand to flick a fly away from his nose and mouth. He studied the grouping of the shots, calculating just how much the gun was off. Around six inches high at a quarter mile. Not more than three inches right. To most men it would have seemed like brilliant shooting, but those kind of tolerances weren't good enough for Herne. Not firing at a stationary target in perfect conditions of visibility. The margin was too great. When he got back to Stow Wells he'd walk along to the smithy and see whether he couldn't do something to fix the Sharps himself.

'Louanne!' he shouted again.

The high walls of the arroyo bounced the name back to him. For the first time the shootist felt a faint prickling of concern. Even if she'd fainted, the whore should have recovered by now. Should have heard him calling her. Should have answered him.

Unless she was teasing. Hiding and waiting for him so

that she could jump out on him. That might be it. She'd joked about not having her drawers on.

That might be it.

But there was still the gut-feeling that something was wrong. Herne cocked the Sharps again, moving cautiously forwards.

Looking for the girl.

The cool walls closed around him and the noise of the wind faded away to a total silence. It was so quiet that he could hear the hissing of the blood as it raced through his skull. Each step he took the noise of his boot-heels grating among the stones was like harsh thunder.

'Louanne!' he tried once more.

Herne was a cautious man by nature. And walking into a silent canyon after a vanishing girl heightened all his senses. His finger was tight on the trigger of the Sharps and his eyes raked the fallen boulders that were scattered all along the sides of the ravine.

Thirty paces ahead of him there was a sharp bend in the arroyo, almost at right angles. He closed in on it, moving slower. Tension building.

Twenty paces.

Ten.

'Louanne!'

It was a box canyon. As he rounded the corner he saw that there was nowhere else to go. The sides opened out, leaving a natural arena fifty yards wide, with broken rocks piled all about.

He saw the girl immediately. Knew that it wasn't a game.

Louanne lay on her back, to the left of the canyon, legs spread wide.

Her throat had been slit open.

Jed caught the sound of movement and began to turn, just as the three Chiricahua braves came rushing at him.

10

They were young men and they were ambitious. Eager for glory. The honour of taking this solitary white man. They'd watched from the depths of the canyon, peering out and seeing the way Herne had consistently hit the big cactus with his long gun. All of them wanted that long gun for they had never seen such shooting. Such accuracy. With a rifle like that any one of them would have immediately become a man of importance. A warrior that even Mendez himself would look up to and respect.

And to personally slay the owner of such a gun would also bring great honour.

They were young men, out on a scouting party, a few miles ahead of the main band.

To kill the white woman had been easy. Taking her from behind. It had been Two Knives who'd done it. Creeping behind her, silent as a midnight ghost. One arm locking around her as she sat and waited. A hand tight over her mouth, pulling her back so that her terrified eyes stared straight into the sun. The blade of one of his twin knives drawn deep and hard across her neck, the edge grating on bone.

Louanne died in utter fear, blinded by the bright Arizona sun.

As she lay, legs part, the three young braves had sniggered at her exposed sex, making obscene gestures, one to another. Two Knives privately regretted that he'd killed her so quickly. She was pretty, little older than he was. But very skinny.

83

Then the white man was coming, holding that magical rifle. Walking into their trap. Each of them was desperate to be the killer of the shootist and they agreed that they would not use their own guns or bows.

'There would be no honour in such a death,' said Two Knives, and the others agreed.

They were young men, inexperienced in the arts of fighting, and that saved Herne's life in that first, desperate charge. All three Chiricahua boys came at him together, jostling each other in their eagerness to count coup on the white man with the greying hair.

As he spun round Jed squeezed the trigger of the Sharps, firing from the hip. Not even bothering to see where his shot went, reversing the rifle to use it as a club. There was no time to draw the Colt, held in its holster by the thin leather retaining thong.

The bullet went low.

Low, but straight.

Striking the leading warrior near the top of his right thigh, almost in his groin, ripping through his breech-clout. Striking the femur, then angling sideways and ripping, a distorted hunk of lead, into the young man's genitals.

He screamed once, the impact kicking him over to his right. Dropping his knife, both hands going to the wound, trying to squeeze away the white agony.

Herne glimpsed the Apache fall, but the fight was barely begun. His attempt at a clubbing blow to the head of the second Indian missed as the boy darted and feinted, the Sharps missing him by a finger's breadth. Two Knives came in behind his friends, shocked at the speed of the white man's response. Nearly falling over the tumbling figure of his shot brother.

Herne managed to swing the long, heavy rifle a second time, using it to counter the thrust of Two Knives, who came in at him with his weapons gripped low in both hands, ready for the upwards thrust of the skilled knife-fighter.

'Bastards,' breathed the shootist, not wasting his energy on shouting. Talk was useless.

And the price for inaction was colossal.

The groin-shot boy was rolling around, screaming, mind locking out everything but his own wounding.

The younger of the Chiricahua braves came in a third time, parrying the rifle with his forearm, wincing at the sharpness and power of the impact. Managing to duck and slice sideways at Herne's stomach. The shootist heard the whisper of sound as the tip of the knife hacked open the front of his shirt, drawing a slivered thread of blood from his flesh.

'Close, son,' he said, quietly.

Two Knives started to circle around the big man, hoping to take him from behind. Already he was regretting that they had chosen the path of honour rather than that of safety. They could easily have killed the white man from cover.

But now. . . .

'Now,' hissed Jed, weaving the rifle around his head in a lethal figure of eight. Conscious of the boy coming up at his back. Knowing that the longer this went on, the less good his hopes were. They were younger and fitter than he was and they would inevitably wear him down. You didn't get to live long taking chances, but this might be one time to do it.

He turned on his heel, keeping his balance like a great cat, as though he was about to attack Two Knives. Who stepped instinctively back a pace. The other young brave checked himself, standing still. Herne carried on swinging the rifle, suddenly letting it go, scything through the air and striking the Apache across the knees.

Herne caught the brittle noise of cracking bone and the young warrior fell like a poleaxed steer, rolling in the dirt alongside the first of the Chiricahua.

Two Knives couldn't believe it.

Both down.

One hit where he knew he would not live. The other with a broken knee, helpless to do anything but cry out and crawl away as best he could.

The white man stood motionless, without a weapon to his hands, while Two Knives had both his blades out and ready. Jed made a move towards his pistol, but the Apache saw it and immediately closed with him, yelping his anger. Hoping his fear would not make him lose control of his body and foul himself.

'Die!!' he screamed.

Herne saw there was no chance of sliding out the Colt. He went forward to meet the boy, gripping his wrists with all his great strength, rolling him sideways, kicking at him. Heaving him away to one side, close by the sprawled and bloody corpse of Louanne.

Two Knives gathered himself for another attack, deciding on more caution. He saw the white man was reaching down towards his boot, as though he might have hurt his ankle, and the boy grinned. It would go his way. Crippled, the white man would be easy slaying.

The Apache boy was good. Herne expected that. But, by God he was fast! In with his two skinning knives snaking out at Jed. He winced away, feeling one of the blades nick him across the side of the face, the other catching him on the outer, fleshy part of his left arm.

Two Knives was good.

Herne was better.

In a special sheath in his right boot he carried a razor-edged, needle-tipped Civil War bayonet. His hand gripped the taped hilt and drew it out, hacking up at the Indian with devastating speed and violence.

The boy never even saw it. There was the faintest flicker of reflected light as Herne drew the bayonet. That was all. Then a fiery sensation in his throat. Liquid, warm across his naked chest and arms. He reeled away, the knife falling from his left hand. Staggering. Dropping the other knife. Seeing blood bright in the shadows, pattering in the dry earth around his soft leather boots.

So much blood.

'So much blo . . .'

He died.

Jed looked round, seeing that the Apache boy he'd shot with the fifty-calibre rifle was still rolling over and over, hugging himself, tied into his own suffering. Oblivious to everything else.

The third of the young warriors had disappeared.

'Can't have gotten far,' grunted the shootist, flexing his fingers, making sure that the cut on his arm hadn't done any damage. But the wound was only shallow, superficial. It was bleeding freely, dappling the sleeve of his shirt, but that would soon stop. There was also a smaller amount of blood trickling down his face from the cut on his right cheek. Herne had done worse to himself shaving.

Suddenly there was the clatter of hooves from above him. 'God damn!' he breathed.

From the trail in the dirt it was obvious that the crippled Chiricahua had managed to haul himself up a hidden path and reached his pony. If they were a scouting party for Mendez then it would be a good idea to stop the boy from giving his news. If none of his scouts returned, it might at least slow the war-chief down some.

Herne stooped and picked up the heavy rifle, ignoring the weeping of the gut-shot boy, and ran quickly along the canyon. Following the trail, seeing the narrow path that snaked up the walls of the ravine. Reaching the top as the thundering of the animal's hooves was fading in the distance, away to the north. The boy was already close on three hundred yards off, leaning low over the pony's neck, his broken left leg trailing on its flanks.

It took the shootist only a couple of seconds to eject the spent cartridge from the Sharps and slide in a fresh round. Quickly adjusting the sights, bracing the long gun against his shoulder. Setting his finger on the trigger and steadying his breathing after the short, sharp climb.

The Apache was a touch over four hundred paces off,

riding hard, almost invisible behind a seething curtain of spiralling red dust.

'Six inches high. Three right,' he said, remembering the target shooting at the saguaro cactus.

Bringing the sights in line. Holding his breath. Firing.

Stepping immediately to one side, automatically reloading the Sharps. Watching for the effect of the bullet.

It was a perfect shot.

Striking the galloping man precisely in the back. Three fingers left of his spine and three fingers below the sharp angle of the shoulder-blade. As he was leaning forwards it burst through the muscular walls of the boy's heart, clean through, between the ribs and exiting out of the left side of his chest, cutting a bloody gouge along the neck of his pony.

It kicked and reared, spilling the dying brave in the dirt. Herne stood, silently watching. Intent on seeing if a second bullet would be needed.

The Chiricahua rolled over twice, arms and legs flung out like discarded bolts of cloth. Then he lay still.

Behind the shootist, at the bottom of the canyon, the last living Indian was still crying out. Herne walked carefully down the path, stopping near the boy, looking down at him. Wondering whether the wound was fatal. Guessing it was, but it would take a long time.

The Chiricahua was suddenly aware of his presence as the shadow of the white man fell across him. His eyes blinked open and he stared up out of eyes that were too blurred with pain to see properly.

Herne shook his head as he saw how young the Indian was. Unlike many whites Jed had never felt any great personal hatred of Indians. Sure there'd been a lot of times that he'd killed them. But that had generally been because they had been trying to kill him. As far as he was concerned, any Indian was much like any white.

Not to be trusted at any time.

That was the safest line of thinking.

He knelt beside the teenage Apache, reaching down to ease the thong off the hammer of the Peacemaker. Drawing the forty-five pistol and thumbing it back. The triple click of the cocking action.

The boy closed his eyes again, lips moving slowly. 'Aid me, my father, in my passing,' he muttered.

'Sure,' said Herne.

Blood wormed down over the Indian's chin, where he'd bitten his tongue in his pain. Jed lowered the handgun, pressing the barrel against the warrior's mouth. Pressing hard to make him part his lips.

The eyes opened again, frightened. Uncomprehending. Gazing into Herne's face, seeing no spark of humanity or warmth. No pity.

'Aid me,' he whispered.

Herne understood something of the Apache tongue and he nodded. 'I will. Open,' probing at the compressed lips with the gun.

The Chiricahua finally opened his mouth and the barrel of the Colt slid easily between the jaws.

Herne turned his face away to avoid the risk of becoming splashed with blood and brains . . . and squeezed the trigger.

The sound of the explosion was oddly muffled, the gun kicking up and breaking the boy's front teeth. The forty-five ripped through the roof of the Indian's mouth, pushing the palate to rags of torn flesh. Up into the frontal lobes of the brain, then punching a great hole in the back of his skull, splintering away a chunk of bone bigger than a grown man's fist.

The body jerked back, legs kicking and jerking like a shot rabbit. The hands clenched and opened. Clenched and opened. The eyes stared up at the deep blue sky. Blood came down the nose and seeped from the open mouth.

Jed replaced the spent bullet, spinning the chamber, reholstering the pistol. Looking round the ravine, shaking his head at the dead body of Louanne.

He didn't waste time on words. She wouldn't hear them. Time was now crucial. If the boys were scouting, then Mendez and the rest of the warriors wouldn't be far behind. Maybe four or five hours. Odds were he'd be coming before sunset.

'From the north,' guessed the shootist.

That was the direction that the boy with the broken leg had been heading. Out into the foothills. That meant Mendez would be coming for the town. If his intelligence was good enough the Apache would know that the town was virtually empty of fighting men. So he'd come on in for the easiest pickings he'd ever dreamed of. And if he came from the north the first thing he'd see would be. . . .

Jed looked to the left. Behind the steep walls of the canyon lay the neat white buildings of the Abernathy Home.

He left the whore's corpse where it lay, the two dead Indians on either side.

The wound in his arm was still bleeding freely and it was almost impossible for him to tie a tourniquet with only one hand. He headed towards the Home, shaking his head and sighing at how weak he was feeling. Blinking at the dazzling light outside the arroyo.

It took a quarter of an hour to make the short distance across rough, broken ground, leaving a trail of dark spots in the sand.

Several of the old men saw him coming and he heard someone yelling out for Miss Lily to come quick. He recognised Ben, standing in the yard, holding a broom.

Another of the old-timers came hobbling up to him, flies gaping open.

'Hey, you're Herne, ain't you? Al's goin' to be mighty pleased. You're wounded.'

'Yeah. Where's. . . .?'

But the old man hadn't finished. 'You know me, don't you?'

The shootist was puzzled, wanting only to get out of the sun and have someone stop the bleeding from his arm. 'No. No, I don't know you. And who's Al?'

'Don't know me! Hell, Herne . . . I'm . . . I'm . . .' The eyes misted and the mouth sagged. 'I'm . . . Jesus, I'm always forgettin' who . . .' The voice faded and he wandered off towards the house.

The main door swung open and Jed saw a woman he recognised as Miss Lily Abernathy walking briskly towards him. Ben was still watching.

'Hey, who's Al?' asked the shootist. 'And why'll he be glad to see me?'

The old-timer gave a sly grin and winked. 'Why? 'Cos Al Carson says he's your Pa, Mister Herne. That's why.'

11

'My father?'

'Keep still.'

'But I need to know, for Christ's sake! I mean . . . my father.'

'Will you keep still so that I can tie this bandage properly around your arm.'

'It's fine.'

The woman sniffed as though he'd broken wind at a social tea. 'It most certainly is not fine, Mister Herne.'

'It's . . .'

Miss Lily Abernathy favoured him with her most steely glare. 'I say that it is not better. I have nearly done with bandaging you. A great deal of blood was lost, Mister Herne.'

'Happens when someone sticks a knife in you, Miss Abernathy.'

'And I do not wish to experience your trail-drive, drifter attempts at sarcasm, if you would be so kind as to cease them.'

'Yes, Ma'am.'

'There. It's done.'

'Thank you. Can I talk some now?'

Miss Lily Abernathy was a poem in black bombazine. Hat of black feathers nodding as she moved around the cluttered parlour where Herne had been taken. She washed the blood off her hands in a white porcelain basin and dried them on a spotless linen towel.

'You may. You say that we are at some risk from an

attack from that rapscallion, Mendez?'

'Yes. I killed three of his young bucks. I figure they was scoutin' this way to . . .'

'Were,' she interrupted.

'What?'

'I said they were.'

'Were what, Ma'am?' Herne was becoming thoroughly confused. It was like meeting the head-mistress of some awesome girls' finishing school. Again, for a fleeting moment, his thoughts returned to dead Becky.

'You said they was. I was merely attempting to improve your abysmal grammar.'

'Well, I surely thank you for that, Miss Abernathy. Mendez and his gang of Chiricahua *are* comin' this way. I figure for them gettin' here around sundown.'

The woman came and sat down on an over-stuffed sofa across from him. She crossed her ankles and tapped one finger on her perfect teeth. She was certainly every bit as handsome up close.

'We have time to get into town?'

Herne nodded. 'Sure. But I don't . . .'

'Because all of the able-bodied men have gone off on a wild-goose chase after those robbers.'

She was also very quick on the uptake. 'That's correct.'

'I know it is, Mister Herne. There is no point in wasting precious time on idle chatter.'

The shootist felt like he'd just been rapped over the knuckles with the edge of a steel rule.

'We're better here.'

'Perhaps. They said in Stow Wells that you had not gone because you were scared.' She looked across at him with a calm, level gaze. 'I see from meeting you that they were quite, quite wrong.'

'Idle chatter, Miss Abernathy,' he warned, smiling slightly.

'*Touché*, Mister Herne.'

'I have to ask about my father.'

'Albert Carson. One of the saddest cases among so many.'

'Carson? Carson, like the Pass?'

'Yes. Why?'

'I was born in Carson Pass.'

'Would you recognise . . .?'

Herne shook his head. 'Ma died bearing me. I never even saw my father that I recall. He disappeared into Indian country in the fall of 'forty-four.'

'And then?'

'Nothing, Ma'am. Not a word. Nothing. I always figured him for dead.'

'Perhaps he is. Albert Carson is not . . . how shall I say? Not entirely reliable as far as matters of thé memory go.'

'Ninety cents in the dollar?'

'Perhaps no more than fifty cents, and that on one of his better days. He has been with us now for some four years. A delightful man.'

'And he says he's my Pa.'

'He does. Always has. It is, perhaps the one consistent detail in his blurred past. He is very proud to be the progenitor of such a notorious killer, Mister Herne. Very proud.'

Herne was used to that kind of bitterness. A town asked you in to rid them of some scum that was terrorising the community. You did it for them and they drew away when the blood started spraying around. After that all they wanted was to throw your money in the dirt and watch you ride away out of their lives.

That was the way of it.

'I'd best get started on organising some sort of defence.'

'Defence, Mister Herne! I don't. . . . Come in, my dear.'

Andreanna Abernathy was still wearing the same clothes that Herne had seen when the couple had come into Stow Wells. The simple black jacket in soft leather, over a pleated, divided skirt in plain black material. And the same riding boots with tiny silver spurs. That jingled

as she walked across the room and shook Jed by the
hand, firm and strong as most men.

'You're Herne the Hunter.'

'Miss Andreanna.'

'Your father is waiting for the chance to talk to you.
We can arrange a private room for them, can we not,
Mama? In the visitors' wing.'

'Be glad to talk, Ma'am, and find out whether this old
guy is really. . . .' He found that he couldn't bring himself to say the words. Not after so many years of total
certainty that his father must be dead. 'Things to do first,
less'n we all aim to end up deader than beaver hats.'

The daughter smiled at him. 'Oh, the Indians. You
believe they will attack us.'

'I surely do. They'll come this way. And when they
come for town they'll stop off and take us first. Figure us
for a fine fat steer to have its throat opened up.'.

'They would attack a charitable institution like this one
and risk harming such sweet old men and two utterly
defenceless women?' asked Miss Lily.

Herne wouldn't have called either of them 'defenceless'
but he let that pass.

'Sure would. I guess Chiricahua language doesn't have
much to do with charitable institutions. Fact they're old
men makes them easier to kill. Fact you think you're
defenceless makes it a whole lot easier to strip you and
rape you and then take you in as servants for the rest of
the tribe.'

'Servants!' exclaimed Andreanna. 'That would be just
intolerable, Mama.'

'I'd have figured the rapin' was worse, but that's just
my point of view,' said Herne. 'Fact is, I'd best get up and
about.'

'Should we not try and get everyone into town with the
rest of the folks?' asked the mother.

Herne shook his head. Standing up, feeling that he was
a whole lot weaker from loss of blood than he'd expected
to be. 'There's no men there worth a damn. Frame houses.

Burn easy. No good place to try and defend. This is different. Built a mite like a fortress.'

Lily smiled at him, reaching out and touching him on the shoulder. 'That was the intention of my dear late husband. Colonel Roderick Abernathy. When he decided to found this Home for the poor lost souls who wander this great land of ours.'

'Colonel?' asked Herne.

'In the Confederate States Army, Mister Herne. He rode with. . . . Who is it?' there had been a soft knocking on the door, like a small animal trying to get in.

'Only me, Miss Lily.' It was the old-timer whose memory had given out on him.

'What do you want? Are the Apaches coming?'

'Are they? By God but we'll . . .'

'No, Angus. No. I asked whether they were coming. I see they are not.'

'No. No, Miss Lily. Just wanted Mister Herne here to know I recalled what I done. Led the wagons to the sea. That's what I done. Independence, Missouri. To the sea. That's what I done.'

He stood, eyes bird-bright, waiting for Jed to reply. The shootist nodded at him. 'That's good. Real good.'

'Knowed you'd appreciate that. Knowed you would.' Without another word he turned and shuffled out, forgetting to close the door behind him.

'You think we can defend this place with men like that?' asked Andreanna, mockingly.

'That or nothing. You got guns?'

'Not many. My daughter and I each carry a small over-and-under derringer for our own protection. A hunting rifle. That is all.'

'Jesus!' exclaimed Herne, disgusted. With no guns his idea collapsed. His immediate reaction was to head for town, get his horse and move on south as fast as he was able.

'There's Papa's collection,' said Andreanna.

'Ah, that is true. My dear late and much loved husband

96

was something of a collector.'

'What kind?'

'Muskets. Entirely muskets.'

'Powder and ball?'

'Ample supplies. He used to fire them for sport.'

'That'll do it. With old men like this there couldn't be better than muskets.'

'There is also a brace of flintlock pistols.'

'Better than nothin'. Then let's to it.'

It was like the Widow Abernathy had said. Her late husband, the dear Colonel Roderick, had built up a fine collection of muskets. Concentrating exclusively on the 1835 Model. There were five dozen, neatly chained in polished beech racks, every gun gleaming and oiled and ready to fire.

'Pretty, Ma'am. But I'd have traded them all in for a half dozen Winchesters.'

'The men can use them, surely?' But the question showed her own doubt.

'Should be. Most of 'em must have fired muskets like this when they were younger.'

There was a card pinned to the end of the long rack of weapons. In a trim hand that Herne guessed must have been the late Colonel's was written the basic specifications for the guns.

'The Model 1835 Flintlock Musket. The calibre is ·690 minimum bore. The barrel is precisely forty and two inches in length. The average weight is nine pounds and nine and a half ounces. The trigger guard is of iron with finger ridges on the trigger plate at the rear side of the guard. The stock of the musket is of polished black walnut. The length is fifty and four and three-quarters of an inch and the model has a high, unfluted comb.'

'Mighty accurate, your late husband,' said Herne. 'Powder and ball?'

'Locked in that room there. Here is the key.'

It was a properly constructed magazine, with stone

walls and no windows. The powder in canvas bags and the ball in brass-bound oak boxes. Another of the Colonel's notices was on the white-painted wall.

'For the muskets a bullet weight of four hundred and twelve grains is ideal. Powder charge of one hundred and ten grains. Flints are already in place in the goosenecks of the muskets. A brace of Kentucky smoothbore pistols is to be found in the armoury, locked in a side cupboard.'

'That's all we need, Ma'am. Best get all the men together and bring the stock in out of the fields around. I'll walk about with your daughter, if I might, and make arrangements where we can defend best.'

Lily Abernathy nodded her agreement. 'Very well. I see that you have military training, Mister Herne. Were you in the War?'

'Yes, Ma'am, but I don't care to talk of it.'

'I understand. I'll busy myself. Yes, Ben, what is it?'

The old man had his Walker Colt tucked in his belt and he was spluttering with excitement at the prospect of being able to use it.

'They're comin', Miss Lily. I seen dust, maybe five, eight miles off.'

'You got good eyes, Ben,' said Herne.

'I can see an eagle shit at a mile, Mister Herne . . . beggin' your pardon, Miss Lily and Miss Andreanna. Just don't see so good close up.'

'That'll be Mendez,' sighed Herne. 'Way faster than I figured. They'll be here in a half hour or so. We sure got to get moving, ladies.'

Lily ran out, hoicking her skirts up to the middle of her shapely calves, calling some of the old men to help her arrange some sort of defence and move the animals.

'I'll come with you, Mister Herne,' said Andreanna. Jed noticed that her voice was trembling and that she was biting her lip with the tension. She was holding a scrap of handkerchief, fingers white, almost tearing it to shreds.

'Sure. I want some windows sealed and shuttered where possible.'

'Yes.'

'The guns broken out and handed around to any man you think capable of firing it. But no powder or ball. I want to talk to them all first and try and get it done by numbers. Safer that way.'

One of the old men suddenly appeared around the corner of the corridor, standing still in front of them, waiting as if he had something to say. Herne wondered whether it might be a report that Mendez was closer.

'Mister Herne?' he began, hesitantly.

'Yeah. What is it?'

'Jedediah Herne? Jedediah Travis Herne?'

'Sure. Are . . .?' He looked more carefully at the old-timer. The man was skinny, wasted, a long scar seaming his forehead and running down across the side of his temple towards his ear. The hair was thin, silvered. The body inside the standard Home's uniform of dark blue breeches and cream loose-sleeved shirts was frail.

The old man's eyes were dark, brown, set deep in hollowed sockets. Fixed on Herne's face with a desperate longing.

'Yeah. Jedediah . . . I'm . . . I'm . . .' and he began to weep.

12

Albert Carson was so distressed that any conversation was impossible. Ben appeared at his elbow and took him gently away. Herne found himself unable to speak. Unable to make contact. Only when the two old men were almost out of sight he called after them. 'I'll . . . I'll get to talk in a whiles.'

'Is that . . .?' began Andreanna. But the shootist interrupted her.

'How the Hell would I know! I never fuckin' met him, did I?' Realising that his own reaction and out of character obscenity showed his own lack of balance. He thought of apology and changed his mind. 'Hell, let it pass, Ma'am.'

'Albert Carson could be your father, could he not?'

'I don't . . . Yeah, I guess he could. Pa's name was Albert. Albert Jedediah Herne. He looks the kind of age.' He hesitated. 'We'll see. If'n we all get through the next couple of hours, we'll see. But let's get to it!'

There were twenty-two old men, ready and willing to hold a musket. Albert Carson was not one of them, lying on his bed, sobbing uncontrollably. The few stock were all brought in, and the windows barricaded. Colonel Roderick Abernathy had done his building well. Stone so that fire was no hazard. Shutters that closed from inside, with narrow slits for rifles. Only two doors, both easily commanded from windows.

If only the old-timers did their work well Herne felt confident that they could make themselves such a difficult prey for Mendez and his Chiricahua to swallow that they might pass on by.

Jed had them lined up in the main entrance hall, standing facing him. He held one of the muskets and the powder and ball were laid out in front of him.

'I killed me three Pawnee before breakfast with one of them little beauties,' came a reedy, piping voice from the second row.

'That is good to know,' smiled Lily Abernathy. Herne was impressed with the way that the middle-aged woman was maintaining her calm in the face of possible death. Her daughter was much less in control, going around at the request of the shootist to check on food and water supplies in case of need. It was highly unlikely that they would have to hold out under siege from the Apaches. That wasn't the way of the Chiricahua. But it gave the girl something to do to take her mind off her own growing terror.

'Who said that?' asked Jed.

'Me,' said the same voice. It was the old man with the shattered memory. The one who'd led the wagons to the sea.

'What do you call him?' Herne whispered. 'Him. The man with no name.'

'He sometimes thinks his name was Joseph. And he was born in Cardiff in Wales in England. So we call him Joseph Wales. He answers happily to that.'

'Fine. Joseph. Come out here and show us what you can do about loading her up. I'll kind of talk around what you do so the others recall it.'

'Sure. Sure, Mister Herne. Be mighty proud to. Good to know us old-timers ain't all washed up on the . . .' Again his mind faded away and he lost the thread of the sentence, the words drifting off into the stillness.

'Go ahead.'

Joseph Wales picked up the musket, looking at the table for the familiar ammunition. Starting the longish and complex operation of loading the gun.

Herne watched him carefully, seeing to his surprise that the old man was in perfect control. Every move slotting into the next. Herne guessed that it was like learning to swim. Once you'd done it, then you never forgot how to do it.

'Half-cock the hammer. Snap open the frizzen. There's the priming-pan. Show them, Joseph. Fine.'

'Hell, we don't need these baby lessons, Herne,' moaned Paddy.

'Some don't. Some do. Carry on, Joseph. Get out one of those ready-made cartridges. Musket in your left hand and cartridge in the right. Or the other way if you're . . . Go on. Bite off the end of the paper. Pour around . . . What is it?'

There was a hand up at the back from a man he didn't know. 'Mister Herne,' came a mumbling voice.

'Yeah?'

'I don't have no teeth, Sir.'

There was a ripple of laughter. 'Then you put down the damned gun and tear off the end. Pour around ten grains of powder in the priming pan. Snap shut the frizzen. Very good, Joseph.'

Though his hands were trembling, Jed guessed that it was age, and a certain tension at finding himself unexpectedly at the centre of the stage.

'Tip the rest of the powder down the barrel. Try not to spill any. Lose power if'n you do. Drop in the ball and wad up the paper from the cartridge. Shove that after the ball.'

A man came tottering into the room, waving his arms, the loose cream sleeves flapping like the top-gallants of a clipper rounding Cape Horn.

'Gettin' closer, Mister Herne!!' he yelped, voice creaking with excitement.

'How long?'

'Can't be more than ten minutes.'

'Keep tellin' me,' replied the shootist. 'I figure they'll hold up a while around a quarter mile off. Kind of reconnoitre. Go back and watch.'

'How 'bout a gun?'

'You'll get one in time. Go on.'

The oldster disappeared like a rat behind an arras, hands still waving as though he was conducting some inaudible piece of music. Herne wondered whether any of the old men might not just plain drop dead from all the disturbance to their usual calm routine.

'Where did you get to, Joseph?'

'Just pushed the paper in, Colonel.'

'That's right. Go on. Get the ramrod and push the ball and wadding down as far as you can towards the breech. Real hard. That's all.'

'Can I . . .?'

'No. Don't cock it yet.' Herne didn't want the room filled with over-enthusiastic old men all loading and cocking their muskets. The result could easily be a massacre if someone accidentally touched a trigger.

'Can we start?' asked Ben.

'Sure. And keep that damned cannon of a Walker in your belt until they get real close.'

'Hell, Mister Herne. I don't have but two bullets for it.'

'Don't start thinking about saving them for my daughter or myself,' said Miss Lily Abernathy with a thin smile. 'We are capable of looking after ourselves, Benjamin.'

'Sure, Ma'am. Sure.'

'Get to it,' urged Herne. 'We got more muskets than sharpshooters. Load them all. Careful. Then those that can't fire or don't see too well can stand by and be a loader.'

He stepped back out of the way, bumping into Lily Abernathy. His arm brushing against her bosom. Surprised at the softness, expecting that she would be tightly corsetted. And she made no effort to move away from the pressure, looking sideways at him and smiling.

'Why, Jedediah. . . .'

'I'm sorry, Ma'am.'

103

'I once met a fine young officer in the United States Cavalry. Name of Brittles.'

'Nathan? I knew him.'

'The same. He used to tell me that to apologise was a sign of weakness. I do not think you are a weak man, Jedediah, so please do not feel any necessity for apologising to me for that touch.'

There was nothing that the shootist could think of to say. She was a marvellously attractive woman and there might be time.

And they might all be dead.

'We might all be dead in an hour, Miss Lily,' he said.

'And maybe not, Jedediah.' She smiled. 'But you are correct in your attitude. First we shall fight against the heathen and then . . . then we shall have to wait and we shall see what we shall see.'

The building was as secure as they could make it. Every window had its marksman and behind every man there was another, ready to hand over a loaded musket and reload the spent weapons.

The front door had two guards on it and the rear door was watched by one of the oldest men there. His name was Josiah Fisher and he was armed with one of the pistols. Herne was worried about Fisher, who seemed utterly vague about what was happening and what he was supposed to be doing.

Adreanna Abernathy had placed him there. Explaining to Herne that it was the position that the old man usually took.

'He's doorman, you see, Mister Herne. Doorman. That's where he'll feel safe. His job each day is to take charge of that door and let in visitors.' Her voice was fast and high, showing her tension. Herne nodded.

'Sure. That's fine. Where's Al Carson?'

'He's been askin' for you, Jed. Keeps cryin' and sayin' he's found his little boy. I guess that he's lost control some. He's in the room at the further corner of the building. Safe enough. No window there. Along the corridor from the rear door.'

'I'll try and get to see him in a while.'

She was about to walk on when she stopped and looked at the tall shootist. 'Do you . . . do you think that he is truly your father?'

Herne considered the question. 'I just don't know. Right age. Name. Fact he's claimed it. No reason to do that if it wasn't true. I just . . .' he shrugged. 'I just don't know.'

'Here they are!!'

'Eighteen.'

They were ranged in a loose half-circle, sitting their dappled ponies and staring towards the large white building. It was easy to pick out Mendez. Wearing a shirt of flamboyant blue silk, that looked like it might once have belonged to an overweight whore. It was decorated with coloured satins and hung loose outside white cotton breeches.

Herne peered out through one of the slits in the heavy shutters. Weighing up distances and chances. The Indians were around three hundred paces off. The light was showing signs of beginning to fade away towards the east and evening wasn't far off. Jed knew that he could hit Mendez without much difficulty, using his Sharps. But the Chiricahua weren't like some other tribes. Kill an Apache chief and the rest just kept on coming.

There was a temptation to allow the old men to break their own tension by firing off a volley at the Apaches. It would make Mendez realise that he was up against a well-armed fortress and it might make him ride on by.

Or it might make him relish the potential challenge.

The other problem with allowing the occupants of the Home to open fire was that Herne guessed that they were unlikely to make much practice even against close targets. He recalled something he'd once read.

A Colonel Hanger, an officer in the English Army, had

said in about 1815: 'A soldier's musket will strike the figure of a man at eighty paces; it may even be a hundred, but a soldier shall be very unfortunate indeed who shall be wounded by a common musket at one hundred and fifty paces. As to firing at a man at two hundred paces you may as well aim at the moon. No man was ever killed by a common musket at two hundred paces by the soldier who had aimed at him.'

The kick from a charged musket was quite severe, and many of the men were exceedingly frail. The recoil was probably sufficient to put most of them flat on their asses.

Herne decided to wait before ordering any of them to open fire.

At that moment he heard the noise of a shot and a scream of pain.

13

It was the tallest of the old men. An ex-soldier who must once have been a holy terror of his regiment. Nicholas Webb, still at seventy-four standing four inches over six feet and weighing in at around two hundred and seventy pounds.

He had insisted on commandeering one of the two Kentucky pistols, loading it himself with the casual ease of the professional soldier. Cocking it ready for action and sticking it in his belt. Unfortunately the trigger hooked on a jack-knife that also hung from the belt and the hand-gun had discharged.

Now he was lying on the floor, surrounded by most of the rest of the Home's inhabitants, all looking at him, seeming as if half of them were about to pass out on the spot.

'What the . . .?'

'I'm sorry, Mister Herne,' moaned Webb. 'I'm real sorry. I shot myself clean through the middle of the damned foot!'

'Holy Christ! Two of you get him out of the way. Rest of you back to . . .'

He was interrupted.

'Here they come!'

Jed ran to the nearest window, carrying the loaded Sharps rifle in his right hand, wishing that he had the Winchester from the his room in the Inside Straight saloon, back in Stow Wells.

Mendez had heard the sound of the shot. Seeing no

visible effect from it he had concluded that someone inside was feeling edgy and had lost their nerve. That seemed a good enough reason to the Chiricahua leader to whoop his band in towards the white walls of the Home.

They were coming in at a slanting angle, lying low across the necks of their ponies. Herne bit his lip in a sudden burst of anger; the warning shot from Webb had blown away any hope of taking the Chiricahua by surprise. They could have picked off some of them, though he doubted the ability of most of the old-timers to hit a galloping man with the muskets.

Now it was going to be a whole lot harder.

'Don't fire!' he yelled at the top of his voice. 'Wait for the word, and make 'em count!'

He watched through the slit, pushing the long barrel of the Sharps out into the dulling light. The Apaches cast enormous, distorted shadows away to the right as he looked at them. Mendez was in the lead on a wiry pinto, heeling at it to swing it from side to side, making himself a more difficult target. He was good. Good enough for Herne not to risk a shot at him. Picking instead one of the other warriors to the left.

'Wait for the word!' he called out again, hoping that his voice would carry through the almost visible tension that filled the Home.

'Wait!'

The nearest of the Indians was within a hundred paces and Herne instinctively felt that he could hold back the old men no longer. An impressive volley that missed was better than ragged shooting.

'Now!!'

The house seemed to rock with the explosions. Black powder smoke billowed from every window, making it look as though the entire building had caught fire. Herne waited a moment before squeezing the trigger of the Sharps, peering through the slit and having the satisfaction of seeing the Indian he'd aimed at throw up his arms and topple lifelessly from his mount.

But as far as he could see none of the other attackers had gone down. Then he saw a pony stumble and fall, throwing its rider clean over its neck. But the warrior was up and running, dodging like a scared jack-rabbit, diving for cover into a narrow draw some fifty paces from the northern flank of the house.

'Get reloading,' yelled Herne, hearing the first sounds of bullets striking the walls of the Home, clattering against the shutters and rapping on the doors as the Apaches circled around, firing their rifles under their ponies' necks.

Jed decided that he could do best by moving around and keeping an eye on the old men, encouraging them and urging them on. Making sure they were reloading and checking any tendency to panic. He'd seen enough action during the great War between the States to know that even the hardest of soldiers might lose his nerve in the grim whirling reality of action. One third of the muskets picked up after Shiloh had either been loaded incorrectly, or carried several charges, or in many cases still had the ramrod jammed down the barrel.

'Steady, men,' he called as he walked through the main hall.

Josiah Fisher was sitting on a chair near the rear door, listening to the sounds of fighting from outside. Twice shifting in his seat as bullets thudded on the heavy oak of the door.

'Knock, knock, Mister Herne,' he cackled. 'Like bein' porter on the gates of Hell, ain't it?'

Herne nodded and hurried by. Pausing to look in at the room where his . . . his father? Could it be? Where the man lay who called himself Al Carson.

The old man rolled over on the narrow bed, looking towards the door. Blinking at the shadowy figure he saw there. The scar across his head stood out livid and fresh.

'That you, Jed?'

'Yeah. How are you doin'?'

'Not so dusty, son. Not so dusty.'

Herne looked down at him. Wondering. Wondering how he felt about it. 'You truly figure you're my father?' he asked, finally.

'I know it, son. Been many a mile of wanderin'. Here and there. Times I been places I don't recall. So many chilly winds.' He shuddered at the cold memories that jostled in his mind. 'I been all round, pushin' on like the headlight on a west-bound train. I heard lots of you. Came close to seein' you once.'

'I can't stay,' said the shootist, hearing voices yelling out for ammunition.

The old man smiled, a tear still glistening on the lined cheek. 'Hell, boy, I know that. Duty calls. Save us all, huh?'

'Hope so.'

'I'm glad, Jed. Real glad.'

'Yeah.' Pausing in the doorway. 'So am I.'

'Even losers, son.'

'What?'

'Get lucky some time. Even losers like me.'

One thing that Colonel Roderick Abernathy had sadly neglected in his building was the numerous walls that scattered and snaked around the Home. Low stone they gave the attacking Chiricahua ample cover once they'd slid off their ponies, darting in and out, snapping off shots at the defenders behind their rifle-ports.

But the spirits inside were high. Ben had succeeded in winging one of the warriors, tumbling him like a ham-strung gelding. Three other men firing at the wounded Indian and all claiming credit for the kill. Herne had to break up the argument as they'd all left their firing positions to continue their high-pitched wrangling.

He saw Paddy, mechanically taking a musket from another oldster, pointing it, and firing. Keeping up a low chant to himself.

'One went high,
One went low.

And where the fuck
Did the third one go?'

Repeating the little verse over and over again, where he'd dredged it up from the Lord-knows-what long-past battles.

Miss Lily Abernathy was standing serenely in the centre of the big kitchen, bandaging the hand of one of the old men who'd caught his fingers in the lock of a musket. Andreanna was sitting in a bentwood chair in the corner, by the stove, fingers tangling and knotting over each other like a nest of soft pink snakes. Her tongue kept flicking out and licking dry lips and she looked up at Herne as he walked in, eyes blank, seeming that she didn't even recognise him. The shootist had seen enough fear in his life to know that the daughter was right on the ragged edge of panic.

'How is it progressing, Jedediah?' asked the other woman. 'Goes the day well?'

'Well enough,' replied Herne, dipping a metal ladle into a bowl of water and taking a mouthful. Swilling it around his mouth and spitting it into a waste bucket near the window.

'Will we . . . will we beat the devils?' asked a voice from the chair. A voice so hollow and frail that Herne had to look round to make sure it really was the brisk and efficient Miss Andreanna Abernathy, Matron of the Home.

'Sure, Ma'am,' he replied, catching the eye of Miss Lily. 'Sure. They're stuck out there and they can't get in at us. No way at all. Doors are locked and barred.'

'How many of the ruffians have we managed to harm?' asked the mother.

'I guess there's two certain dead. And maybe one or two more harmed.'

'We have not suffered any casualties, have we? Apart from poor Webb and his foot and Michael here with his fingers?'

Herne shook his head. 'Your husband built well

enough. If there was maybe twice the number out there then we could have trouble. But Mendez doesn't have the men to try and carry us with a frontal assault. No, I figure we'll be able to hold them off until they get themselves all tired out with the bother.'

'It's nearly dark,' moaned Andreanna. 'I'm frightened of the night.'

'Shut up, child,' snapped her mother. 'You are a grown girl in your twenties. Not a mewling baby. Get a hold of yourself.'

'I'm sorry, Mama,' replied Andreanna.

'Indeed and so you should be.'

Herne turned away. 'I'll keep moving around the house. Kind of keep an eye on everyone.'

'Are the Indians frightened of darkness, Mister Herne?' asked Andreanna.

'There's some are, Miss. But you hear a whole lot of lies and stories about that. Tales that they fear dying in the night in case their spirits lose their way and can't make it to the hunting grounds of the life beyond.'

'And it is not true?'

'Sure. Some Indians think it. But if there's good enough reason there aren't many tribes won't buckle on down and keep fighting after sunset.'

The Chiricahua had built themselves a fire, just down in dead ground to the east of the building. An hour and a half had passed and the shooting against the walls of the Home had faded away almost to nothing. The defenders were eager to carry on pouring lead out into the darkness beyond their rifle-slits, but Herne walked around and told them to stop shooting.

'Hold fire, men. Save powder and shot. Those who've been shooting can stand down and go to the kitchen for a bowl of soup and some bread. Cup of strong coffee. Those who've been loading take their places on watch.' He was aware of how tired some of the oldsters were looking and realised that he would have to organise some

112

kind of rota for guards if Mendez stayed there all night. And the likelihood was that the Apaches would stay at least until dawn.

'Can I have a sleep, Mister?' asked one old man. Joseph Wales, Herne recognised, through the mask of dark powder that grimed his face. It was like the face of a clown, smudged and pale around the eyes and mouth.

'No. Not yet. Once everyone's eaten then we'll fix up for some to get a rest while others stand sentry. That all right?'

There was a muttered chorus of agreement.

Everything went well. By nine half of the old men were asleep, while their comrades stood by the shutters, occasionally checking out into the darkness. Herne had ordered most of the lamps in the building extinguished, or turned down low. That way the defenders could keep their night-sight a little better.

Jed walked around, uneasy at the calm outside. Wondering what the Apaches were planning. Unable to believe that they would give up this easily. Maybe they'd try to sneak in through a window, or attempt to break in through one of the doors. But there were guards all round. Even Josiah Fisher was still awake in his chair by the more isolated rear door.

Albert Carson . . . or Albert Herne if that was his given name, was asleep, lying on his back in the bed where Herne had left him. The shootist stepped in and looked down at the old, old man for several minutes. Seeing the way sleep and rest calmed out some of the lines of pain and age. The scar no longer throbbed as it had before and the hands were folded across the scrawny chest.

The blanket had fallen away and Herne stooped and pulled it up, tucking it in under the old man's armpits. The movement disturbed him and the eyes blinked open. Seeing Herne and then closing again. The lips moved and the shootist caught the words.

113

'Good to have you back, son. So many years.'

It was a little after midnight. The building had been quiet for some time. Every few minutes the Apaches would fire off a couple of rounds, the bullets rattling the walls or banging on doors or shutters. But it hardly disturbed the sleeping old men. Herne had allowed most of them to stand down. Since there was little chance of Mendez breaking the doors he'd also permitted the two old-timers guarding them to lie down where they were to rest. Josiah Fisher was wrapped in a blanket, cocooned like an Egyptian mummy, by the back door.

Andreanna Abernathy was tossing and turning in a fitful slumber in the kitchen, on a mattress that lay in front of the fire. Her mother had been walking around, some of the time sitting with Herne. Neither of them able – or wanting – to sleep. For some time they'd stood together by the shutters that covered the extreme south-eastern corner of the building, furthest away from the fires of the Apaches.

They'd talked quietly, not wanting to disturb the dozing oldsters around them. Chatting of places they'd been. Matters of no real consequence. Jed found that he liked the woman. Was attracted to her, very strongly.

Wanted her.

But neither of them mentioned the idea of their making love. The only clear hint that she felt the same as he did was when they parted. Lily raised herself on tip-toe and brushed her lips softly against his stubbled cheek.

'I'm going to secure a little rest for myself, Jedediah.'

'I'll wait on through until after dawn.'

'You don't need the sleep?'

'Not so much.'

'On the way I'll look in the rear hall and make sure Josiah is safe.'

The shootist nodded. 'Sure, Ma'am. I hope you sleep well.'

'Thank you, Jed. Thank you.'

He stayed where he was for a few seconds, then decided to follow Lily Abernathy along the corridor, to the silent back of the house.

Suddenly he heard what sounded like the creak of a bolt being drawn and a cool draught of night air whispered past him.

For a frozen moment Herne stood where he was, unbelieving.

Then he started to run.

Knowing that he would be way too slow and way too late.

He was.

14

There were six of the Apaches already in the house, holding rifles and knives.

Herne's eyes raked across the hall, taking in the terrifying tableau. Mendez wasn't among the Chiricahua warriors.

Josiah Fisher still actually had his hand on the main catch of the door, leaning against it. Eyes turned to look towards Herne. Mouth sagging open. Jed saw then that the old man wasn't leaning on the door. He was hanging on it for support. Trying to keep himself upright against the gaping wound in his chest where one of the braves had knifed him.

Lily Abernathy stood in the hall, only a few paces from Herne, eyes staring at the silent group of watching Indians.

Josiah drew in a sighing breath, coughing once, still watching the shootist.

'Fuckin' sorry, Mister Herne . . . Really . . . I heard them at the door. Like faint knockin' . . . Woke me . . . Woke me up.' Herne realised the Apaches were watching the old man and he slipped his right hand down to free the thong off of the Colt's hammer at his belt. 'Heard knockin' so I opened up and let 'em in. I'm real . . .'

His hand slipped and he fell, his frail body making no sound on the stone flags of the hall. Herne tensed himself for the play that had to come. When Miss Lily Abernathy chose to make her move.

Stepping forwards, face white, twin spots of hectic red high on her cheekbones. Heels clicking on the floor. The

116

Indians all backing off a step at the anger blazing in her eyes. She stopped before the nearest of the young warriors and slapped him with all her strength across the face.

'Jesus,' breathed the shootist.

The Apache staggered under the force of the blow, a trickle of blood immediately appearing in the dark shadows under his broad nose. Lily Abernathy began to turn away from him when the man jerked on the trigger of his carbine. The sound of the shot was deafening in the low hallway.

The woman was knocked sideways as though she'd been kicked, hands going out to try and break her fall. The bullet had hit her in the chest, forcing the breath from her. She hit the flagstones in a clumsy, kneeling position, head turned towards the shootist, eyes open and staring in the dim light.

Nobody else was looking at the white man and Herne was able to draw with a fluent ease, hammering five shots into the packed group of young Indians. Seeing three of them fall, one catching a bullet through the skull as he was already falling, the other two gutshot and down. Out of any action there might be still to come.

But the other three were alive and, beyond them, through the open doorway, Herne glimpsed movement. Mendez and the remainder of his war-party. There was no way the Home could now be saved. Herne saw that in a flash of realisation.

He turned and sprinted back along the corridor, yelling at the top of his voice to try and rouse as many of the old men as possible. Knowing as he did so that for many of them it wouldn't be enough time. It took too long to waken men of that age, and the Apaches would be in among them before they were properly warned.

The house was built in such a way that it was possible to get around it by a variety of routes, with rooms that connected with each other in three different directions.

At times of great danger Herne's philosophy for most

117

of his life had been to put his own personal safety above all other considerations.

Not this time.

This time he headed towards the room where his father was sleeping. Not the man who thought he might be Herne's father. In the tension of the Apache attack, Jed realised that it had to be true. Everything was right. There wasn't any reason for any of it to be anything else.

He hurdled across one of the inmates of the Home who was struggling to pull up his breeches, stumbling over a pile of muskets. Dashing into the bedroom and seeing Albert Herne standing in the corner, dressed, holding a broad-bladed butcher's knife in his fist.

'They got in, son?'

'Yeah. Only hope's to get out and away in the darkness yonder.'

'Stay and fight?'

'No. There's around a dozen in the house by now. Can only be a matter of time.'

'I'll slow you down.'

'Don't be so damned foolish. Come on, Pa.'

The old man took a step towards him and then stopped still. 'What'd you say, Jed?'

'I said for you to come on, Pa.'

His father smiled. 'Never figured I'd hear you say that, Jed. Never. Sounds good to my ears and that's a fact.'

Along the corridor Herne could hear the noises of bloody fighting. As he'd feared, the Indians were too swift for the old-timers, who were mostly caught cold and butchered where they sat or lay.

Occasionally there was the sound of a musket being discharged but mostly it was just the yelling. Screaming.

Dying.

'Fire.'

'What?' said his father.

'Fire. I can smell smoke. Sure is time we was goin' out of here.'

His father followed him as he cautiously pushed his

head out of the room, seeing that part of the corridor was deserted. Herne quickly finished reloading his pistol and drew the bayonet from his boot, gripping it ready in his left hand.

'Not that way!'

'What?'

'Other way. There's a cupboard. Leads to a stair. Then the roof.'

'How the Hell do you know 'bout that, Pa?' asked the shootist.

'Old man like me gets a mite nosey, son. But we'd best move out.'

The cupboard was built into an angle of the Home and Herne reached for the handle, finding it was stuck. Pulling harder to try and free it. Finally setting his shoulder to it so that it splintered inwards, sending him flying to his knees in the pitch blackness.

It was one of the biggest shocks in his life when he heard a muffled scream and realised that there was someone hiding inside. A shock that was compounded by receiving a violent kick in the face from a silver-spurred riding boot.

'Jesus,' he exclaimed, feeling something break inside his mouth. There was an electrifying lance of pain and he spat out a mouthful of blood. And something hard that rattled on the stone floor of the cupboard.

'Who's that?' said a voice that Herne scarcely recognised.

'Andreanna?' he asked. 'That you?'

'Yes. Mister Herne. Oh, Jesus. What's . . . what's . . .?' and then the girl collapsed in floods of tears. Mumbling helplessly. 'I didn't know it was you . . . I just kicked out when . . . Oh, God, help us all.'

'God helps them that helps themselves, Miss Andreanna,' said Herne's father, pressing in behind his son and pulling the door shut, closing out some of the noise from the fighting and butchery.

'You knocked my damned teeth out,' coughed the

shootist, reaching inside his own mouth with a probing forefinger. Surprised even amidst that looming danger that there wasn't the usual agony that had been plaguing him for months.

'I'm so sorry, Mister Herne . . .' sobbed the young woman.

'Shouldn't be. I been tryin' to get rid of that son of a bitchin' tooth for a long whiles now. Should thank you.'

'The roof, son,' urged Albert Herne.

'Yeah. Up those steps, Miss Andreanna.'

'I can't.'

'You got no choice.'

'I'd rather stay here and die.'

'Then move out of the damned way and let us through. Here, Pa, give me your hand.'

He felt his father reach out for him, the fingers thin like dried twigs. The grip feeble. The woman sank to her knees and began to cry, inconsolably.

'We can't leave her, Jedediah,' said his father.

'We can't take her. They'll be here in maybe only seconds. Talk costs lives. We go.'

'They said you was a hard man, son. They surely said right.'

'No choice, Pa. We got two hopes. Slim and none. She makes it none if we stay. They'll cut us down like cattle if we don't try and run for it.'

'Please help me!' moaned Andreanna, a disembodied voice in the blackness.

'I tried, lady, I tried,' said Herne, feeling for the steps. Hanging on his father's wrist with his other hand.

'Just wait a while,' she begged. 'Maybe they'll go away.'

'Lady . . . I don't have the time.'

The steps were steep and awkward and Herne climbed them carefully. Helping his father close behind him, ignoring the empty crying of the girl. There was a heavy trap-door at the top and he cautiously pushed it up. The night was black and solid, with no trace of a moon visible through banks of low, scudding clouds. There was enough wind to cover any sounds they were likely to make getting out and he stepped onto the flat roof, tugging Albert after him.

'I'll lower the trap,' he said. 'Chance they won't bother with the steps.'

As he laid it down he glimpsed a sudden light. The door of the cupboard was torn open and he caught a flash of men filling the space. The crying stopped and he heard a sharp, desperate scream from Andreanna Abernathy. A scream that was shut off as he set down the heavy cover. His father said nothing but Jed could feel him trembling as he held his hand again.

The night's deeps wrapped them in tightly and Herne walked carefully across, feeling with his foot for the edge of the roof. Finding it and stopping.

'I'll jump down and then catch you.'

'Sure. Go ahead.'

The air was heavy with the stench of smoke and Herne suddenly saw flames darting out of the windows further along the flank of the doomed Colonel Roderick Abernathy Home. The shooting seemed to have stopped and there was little noise. Above the crackling of burning wood he thought he could maybe still hear the noise of a woman screaming.

Alone.

But he couldn't be certain.

His father drifted down into his arms, light and brittle. Herne didn't dare to hold him too tight in case something broke.

'Thanks, son.' They stood in the darkness for a few moments, gathering themselves ready to walk away towards safety.

Herne figured that Mendez was now unlikely to attack Stow Wells. He had taken reasonable losses and didn't have that much to show for it. Probably a third of his band would be dead or injured and their spirits wouldn't be that high. And he would also have to put scouts out to watch for the returning men of the settlement. Though

Herne had the uneasy feeling that Mendez might already have found the posse and taken a toll of their foolhardiness.

'Ready, Pa?'

'As I'll ever be, son.'

'Then let's go on.'

'Son.'

'Yeah?'

The old man was talking so quietly that Jed could hardly hear him.

'Just to say I'm sorry for all them years. When your Ma died I just kind of . . . kind of fell into pieces, I guess. We was so close and all. I kind of blamed you for her death, Jed. I know it sounds foolish. But. . . .'

'Load of water flowed under the bridge since then, Pa. Just don't take on. I don't blame you for it.'

'You sure? I been no kind of father, runnin' out on you.'

'Hell, Pa . . . That's over now.'

'Yeah. Past's past. Now we can. . . .'

He was interrupted by a Chiricahua warrior erupting from the ground, hurling himself at Jed and knocking him to the dirt. The clouds eased away for a few moments and Albert Herne saw his long, long-lost son on his back with the Apache on top of him. The sliver of moon glistening on the knife that was raised.

The shootist had been so involved in talking with his father that his concentration had slipped and he was taken utterly by surprise. Flat in the dirt with the weight of the Indian on him, helpless.

'Pa!' he cried.

The old man threw himself at the back of the Indian, grabbing at the arm that held the knife, his desperation lending his frail old body a sudden strength. It was enough to get the Apache off Jed, giving him a moment to recover his breath, drawing his own knife.

But that moment was also enough for the brave to react against Albert Jedediah Herne. His left hand gripped the old man by the throat, squeezing, while his right hand, with the sharp-pointed knife, punched at Albert's chest.

Again.

A third time.

Albert Herne wasn't conscious of much pain. Just a succession of blows on his body, and a sudden, ineffable weakness that made him want to lie down and rest. As he fell he saw that his son had wreaked revenge for him.

Rising from the earth like a demon, stabbing the Chiricahua so hard that the point of the bayonet stood out several inches through the cotton shirt at the back. Herne cut a dozen times, maybe more, filled with a lust for blood that misted his eyes and closed his brain to reason. Only stopping when he heard his father call out in a weak voice.

Leaving the raggled corpse of the Apache and kneeling besides the dying old man. Lifting the head from the dust and cradling his father to him. Finding that he was crying. Tears coming to his eyes for the first time in more years than he could remember.

'Don't, son,' said his father. 'Don't. It's over now. Doesn't hurt none.'

'I can . . .' began Herne, knowing the futility of the lie he was about to offer.

'You can't, boy. I know it well enough. I see that old black cloud comin' on down and I knew the race is over. Been good to meet you at last, son.' There was a long silence and Jed thought he was gone, though he could just catch the faint sound of laboured breathing, blood bubbling from torn lungs.

'Son . . . I'm sure glad . . . glad . . .'

This time the silence lasted and Jed's father was dead.

Epilogue

The sun was shining as Jed Herne heeled his stallion along the main street out of Stow Wells.

Far to the north he could make out the charred shell of the Home. The morning was hot and he eased his shoulders against the tightness of his shirt. Unconsciously poking with his tongue at the cavity where his rotten tooth had been.

The little town was in mourning, shades drawn down, nobody on the street. The Sheriff's office was closed. Waiting for someone to take on the job now that Clifford V. Williamson was dead. And the smithy had its doors locked. Big Jim Bissett wouldn't be drawing any more teeth for Stow Wells. He'd come back to town the same way that the lawman and three other members of the posse had. Face-down over his horse, wrists and ankles roped together.

Mendez had caught them cold and come in at night, killing easily. Taking lives and scalps. It had been a costly operation for the little township.

And they'd never found any trace of the missing merchant, J.W. Locke. In fact it would be nearly forty years later that children playing in the foothills would discover the dried skeleton, where the Apaches had killed him the day of the stage robbery.

So, it was all over.

Herne reined in at the gate of the little cemetery that served Stow Wells. There were a whole parcel of new graves there, all dug in the last week. Most with plain wooden markers.

But the reason he'd waited before moving on was the stone head-marker in the corner, where a stunted tree threw a little shade. The last thing he'd been able to do for his father was see him buried right and proper.

Jed dismounted and walked into the graveyard, heels crunching through the dry desert sand. Pausing for a moment, head bowed. Remembering.

Then he stepped away, remounted and rode off to the west, never once looking back.

The sun cut deep shadows in the letters on the stone, making them sharp and easy to read.

'Albert Jedediah Herne, born April 7th, 1809. His heart died with his beloved wife Elizabeth Julia on February 29th, 1844 at Carson Pass. Father of Jedediah Travis Herne. Lived on and died finally at Stow Wells in the Territory of Arizona, July 19th, 1887, giving his life for his son.'

Then there was a space, and one more line of text.

'Even the losers get lucky some time.'

THE END

LONELY ON THE MOUNTAIN by LOUIS L'AMOUR

The Sackett Brothers didn't know exactly what kind of trouble Cousin Logan had got himself into but they knew he needed beef cattle badly. So William Tell Sackett, Tyrel, Orrin and Cap Trountree rode north to the wild country – pushing 1100 head of fat steers across the wide Dakota plains towards the mountains of far western Canada. Past Sioux, past Logan's treacherous enemies, through trails no cattle had ever crossed, the Sacketts drove on. Because the Sacketts stick together – and when you step on the toes of one Sackett, they all come running!

0 552 11668 8 – 95p

THE WHIP AND THE WARLANCE by J. T. EDSON

Having thwarted one scheme to invade Canada from the USA, Belle Boyd, the Rebel Spy, and the Remittance Kid were hunting the leaders of the plot, who had escaped and were plotting another attempt. To help them, they called upon a young lady called Miss Martha Jane Canary – better known as Calamity Jane ... Belle, Calamity and the Kid made a good team, but they knew they would need all their fighting skills when the showdown came. For they leLoup Garou and the Jan-Dark, the legendary warrior maid with the warlance who, it had long been promised, would come to rally all the Indian nations and drive the white man from Canada.

0 552 10964 9 – 65p

YONDERING by LOUIS L'AMOUR

Contains adventures of the sea, of war, of the exotic islands of the East, stories based upon experience and people Louis L'Amour encountered during his early yondering days.

Most of the men and women of YONDERING do not dace their challenge in the old West, yet they summon up courage and strengths that would have stood them well on the American frontier. They discover, as L'Amour discovered in his own past, that in the daily act of survival, each of us conquers his own frontiers.

YONDERING, written with all of the sheer storytelling power that we have come to expect from Louis L'Amour, is a different and very special book.

0 552 11561 4 – 95p

SUDDEN by OLIVER STRANGE

A trio of land-grabbing brothers . . . a crooked town marshal . . . a beautiful woman .. between them, they had the town under their heel. Now they meant to take the whole range, their weapons terror and destruction and murder.

Into this Arizona hell-town the Governor sent Sudden. His instructions were brief: 'Clean it up', he said. 'No loose ends'. One man. A texas outlaw with a badge. Sudden.

0 552 11797 8 – 95p

A SELECTED LIST OF CORGI WESTERNS

J.T. EDSON

☐ 07900 6	MCGRAW'S INHERITANCE No. 17		95p
☐ 07992 8	THE DEVIL GUN No. 21		65p
☐ 10964 9	THE WHIP AND THE WARLANCE No. 86		65p
☐ 11224 0	THE GENTLE GIANT No. 89		75p
☐ 09607 5	THE QUEST FOR BOWIE'S BLADE No. 75		95p
☐ 08065 9	GUN WIZARD No. 32		95p

LOUIS L'AMOUR

☐ 11668 8	LONELY ON THE MOUNTAIN		95p
☐ 11618 1	THE WARRIOR'S PATH		95p
☐ 11561 4	YONDERING		95p
☐ 11838 9	MILO TALON		95p

OLIVER STRANGE

☐ 11440 5	SUDDEN TAKES THE TRAIL		85p
☐ 11797 8	SUDDEN		95p
☐ 11795 1	SUDDEN: MARSHAL OF LAWLESS		95p

JOHN J. MCLAGLEN

☐ 10789 1	HERNE THE HUNTER 1: WHITE DEATH		60p
☐ 11585 1	HERNE THE HUNTER 15: TILL DEATH		85p
☐ 10526 0	HERNE THE HUNTER 5: APACHE SQUAW		65p

JAMES W. MARVIN

☐ 11218 6	CROW 2: WORSE THAN DEATH		75p
☐ 11858 3	CROW 6: THE SISTER		95p